"HOLD IT, COLT!" VIC BARON SHOUTED.

Dan didn't flinch. His eyes stayed on Ric, who was now looking past him toward his older brother. Vic ran around Dan and stood between the two, facing Ric.

"Ric, this hawk is *Dan Colt!*" he said breathlessly.

The younger Baron batted his eyes. "You mean *the* Dan Colt?"

"None other. You get out of the way," Vic said, shoving his brother into the crowd. Wheeling, he faced the tall man and went into his stance. His black flat-crowned hat shaded his dark eyes. "I heard you got bushwacked and dumped in a Kansas hole, Colt," he said.

"You heard wrong," Dan said.

"Good. Your reputation has been a thorn in my gut for a long time," Baron hissed. "Now I can take care of it."

*Don't Miss Other Action-Packed Adventures
by Morgan Hill*

DEAD MAN'S NOOSE

The Dan Colt Western Saga:
Volume I: TWIN COLTS
Volume II: THE QUICK AND THE DEADLY

MORGAN HILL is a relatively new name in the Western field. Born and raised in the West, he's a great storyteller in the tradition of Luke Short, Louis L'Amour, and Zane Grey. His story always rings true, because he's traveled extensively around the West, researching the historical circumstances pertaining to each novel. Morgan Hill lives with his wife in the foothills of the Rockies near Littleton, Colorado.

BOOT HILL BROTHER

MORGAN HILL

A DELL BOOK

Published by
Dell Publishing Co., Inc.
1 Dag Hammarskjold Plaza
New York, New York 10017

Copyright © 1981 by Morgan Hill

All rights reserved. No part of this book may be
reproduced or transmitted in any form or by any
means, electronic or mechanical, including photocopying,
recording or by any information storage
and retrieval system, without the written permission
of the Publisher, except where permitted by law.

Dell ® TM 681510, Dell Publishing Co., Inc.

ISBN: 0-440-10794-6

Printed in the United States of America

First printing—June 1981

CHAPTER ONE

The man on the big black horse drew rein as he crested the gradual rise. The vast, sloping valley spread out before him in a rich farrago of color. In the foreground the town of Green River lay in a blanket of rich grass and clustered trees. The town was bordered on the west by the Green River, which threaded its way southward like a silver ribbon in the Utah sun. To the east was a jagged canyon that had been gouged in the valley floor by some ancient cataclysm. The canyon walls revealed various crusted layers of rugged buff-colored rock lined intermittently with heavy folds of porous rusty-red stone worn smooth by centuries of wind and rain. Straight ahead to the south the craggy peaks of the San Juan Range loomed in purple majesty against the pale blue horizon.

Green River was only a half mile in length, with three streets running north and south. The middle street contained the business section, while the other two were residential.

Dan Colt eyed the town carefully from atop his gelding as he removed his wide-brimmed Stetson and sleeved away the sweat on his brow. The furtive breeze flopped his blond locks, and he hesitated briefly before replacing the hat on his head.

From his lofty perch the tall man could see both cemeteries at the same time. Every town of any size on this wild and raw frontier had two cemeteries. One was the resting place for the town's decent citizens. The other was a dismal plot reserved for the carcasses of outlaws and other worthless transients who happened to draw their last breaths in the immediate area. This nefarious but necessary scar on the face of every town was known as Boot Hill. The ultimate in shame and degradation was to end up in a hole on Boot Hill.

A large black hawk swooped low over horse and rider, rose in a high loop, and disappeared toward the north.

Colt narrowed his eyes against the noonday sun and focused them on Boot Hill. It was windswept and dry and conspicuously barren of foliage. The worn and battered gravemarkers leaned every which way, giving evidence of their total neglect.

Three men were struggling with a knotty pine box, preparing to lower it into a freshly dug grave. Some of the more remote towns never bothered to provide even a cheap pine box for a Boot Hill burial. It was evident that Green River's citizens still had respect for human life—at least enough to supply the bodies of society's outcasts with the dignity of a wooden container.

Colt's gaze skipped over the town and fell on the other cemetery. Ironically a stoop-shouldered group was huddled around an open grave into which they were gently lowering a store-bought coffin. The southernmost cemetery was a sharp contrast to Boot Hill. It was encircled by a white picket fence beneath the partial shade of two giant cottonwood trees. The midspring grass within the fence was a plush green. Flowers adorned some of the graves.

The man on the black horse wondered if there were any connection between the two burials.

Touching the gelding's sides with his spurs, he guided it off the ridge, down the slope. The Boot Hill burial detail paused, shovels in hand, to watch the horse and rider pass by.

The town was typical of numberless others that Dan Colt had visited in his relentless search for his outlaw brother, known as Dave Sundeen. The two were identical twins born of pioneer parents who had been murdered on the trail in eastern Arizona. Dan's pursuit held one purpose: He must track down and capture his twin and turn him over to the authorities at Holbrook, Arizona. Dan had been arrested and sent to Yuma Territorial Prison in a case of mistaken identity.

The many years of separation made it impossible for Dan Colt to prove his twin existed. Neither the arresting officer, nor the judge, nor the jury believed his story. He broke out of Yuma and began the search for Dave Sundeen alone.

Green River was characteristic of the small western town. It was a cluster of drab, unpainted adjoining frame buildings poorly disguised by lofty false fronts. There was the customary assortment of stores, saloons, and eating places.

As Colt rode toward the nearest saloon, a faded sign told him that Green River had a physician who also made a stab at dentistry. The saloons and gambling places always afforded information if Dave had bothered to stop in a particular town. Often Dan did not have to bother asking. If Dave had been there, someone usually spoke up, thinking Dan was the outlaw twin.

Saddle leather squeaked as the tall man dismounted stiffly in front of the Blackjack Saloon. The creak and rattle of a wagon coming toward him from the south end of town met his ears. Not bothering to look up, Dan looped the reins around the hitchrail.

Suddenly a female voice pierced the warm afternoon air.

"Grampa! Stop the wagon! *It's Dave!*"

The last word filtered into Dan's thoughts, automatically raising his line of sight to the skidding wagon. A young girl bounded from the wagon before it had come to a full stop, flung her arms around Dan Colt's slender waist, and laid her head on his chest. "Oh, Dave," she sobbed, "you came back! You came for me!"

As she mingled incoherent words with tearful sobs, Dan touched her back lightly with his palms and looked toward the wagon, which was pulling toward him from across the street. His eyes fell on the elderly man holding the reins. He wore a black suit and tie. The woman seated beside him seemed to be much younger by her posture, but a black veil hid her face. In the bed of the wagon sat another girl strongly resembling the one who at the moment was soaking his double-breasted shirt with her tears. The girl in the wagon was younger. Next to her sat a boy of about fourteen, his wide smile exposing a full mouth of teeth. "Oh boy, Mom," he said to the veiled woman on the wagon seat, "Dave came back!"

One thing was for sure: His brother had been in Green River.

Two wagonloads of people passed slowly. All eyes were on Dan. Someone said, "Looks like he's back." Several riders moved by on horses, all of whom he assumed were in the returning funeral procession. One horse that passed bore a tall, slender man holding a big Bible. The rider smiled and nodded at the man he thought was Dave Sundeen.

The woman on the wagon seat lifted the veil, placing it neatly over the black hat and exposing a lovely face with reddened eyes. Dan knew immediately that she was the mother of the three young ones. He guessed she was about forty.

Smiling warmly, she said, "Dave, why did you come back? You said—"

The girl, clinging to Dan like bark to a tree, lifted her head and looked into his eyes adoringly. Interrupting her mother while tearfully gazing at the tall man, she said, "Mama, you *know* why he came back. I told you he would. He really loves me." Thumping his chest with her head, she added, "Don't you, my darling?"

The elderly man shook his head. "I knew it, Clara. Told you I saw it in his eyes. He's come for Molly Jo!"

Dan Colt's brain was spinning like a runaway merry-go-round. He had to find a way to tell these people he was not Dave Sundeen. Inadvertently the old man came to his aid.

"Where'd you get the big black gelding, Dave? You ain't hardly had time to get into a poker game. What'd you do with the buckskin?"

Here was his chance. The boy also gave assistance to his predicament. "And your clothes! Where'd you get *them* duds?"

"Folks, you have mistaken me for my twin brother. I'm not Dave Sundeen," Dan said hurriedly.

Molly Jo lifted her head from his chest, eyes wide. The old man uttered something Dan could not make out. "Dave, what are you doing?" Molly Jo asked.

"I am not Dave, little lady," Dan said, his voice soft. "My name is Dan Colt. Dave and I are twins."

"If you're twins, how come your last name isn't Sundeen?" the girl said, disappointment in her eyes. She pushed herself away from him. "Why did you come back?" she snapped. "If you didn't want me, why didn't you just keep going? Why this twin-with-different-last-names business? Why—"

"Hold it . . . *Molly Jo*, is it?" Dan was groping.

"Oh, Mama," she said, turning toward the wagon.

"Ma'am," Dan said pleadingly to the mother, "I am telling you the truth."

"He never said anything about having a twin," she said with a hint of distrust in her eyes.

Dan pushed the Stetson to the back of his head with a heavy sigh. "This is going to sound crazy, ma'am," he said, blinking his sky blue eyes, "but he doesn't know about me."

Clara's face drew tight. "Now look, mister—"

"Ma'am," Dan interrupted, "you look very tired. I can see that you've just buried someone dear to you. . . ."

The woman raised her hand to her forehead.

"I can see that my brother has involved himself with your family. May I come home with you? You can fill me in on the whole story and I will tell you about Dave and myself."

"One thing about it, Clara," said the old gentleman, patting her shoulder, "if he ain't Dave, he shore is his twin. Sounds like he's tellin' the truth to me."

Clara daubed at fresh tears, then straightened. Lifting her chin, she said, "You're right, Gramps." Looking into Dan Colt's pale blue eyes, she said, "Forgive us, Mr. Colt. We just buried my husband. We've all been under a heavy strain. Please do follow us home."

Molly Jo climbed into the wagon bed, her head hung low. Dan swung astride his mount and rode beside the wagon. *Maybe my luck is changing,* he thought to himself. *Dave might have told these people where he was heading.*

The wagon rolled north out of Green River. As they passed Boot Hill, Dan noticed the fresh mound of dirt where the men had been working earlier. The cemetery was now deserted.

Just past Boot Hill the wagon made a left turn and rattled westward for about ten minutes. They passed two ranches on the way. At the third one the wagon veered off the road and headed for a cluster of buildings that was half-hidden by a heavy stand of trees.

The old man pulled the wagon to a halt near the back door of the freshly painted house. Dan noted the outbuildings all bore the same white paint as the house. The barn was only about a third painted. The remaining two thirds were a sunbleached dull brown.

Dan dismounted and helped Clara from the wagon. He stepped to the rear and offered his hand to Molly Jo as the boy dropped to the ground. Molly Jo lifted her nose, saying coldly, "I'll manage." She followed her brother.

Dan smiled at the younger girl and said, "May I help you, miss?"

She gave him a pleasant look and nodded, extending her arms. Dan judged Molly Jo to be about nineteen or twenty. The younger girl appeared to be about seventeen. It was not until he eased her down and she started for the house that he noticed she walked with a heavy limp.

"Please come in, Mr. Colt," said Clara. The girls had already entered the house. The boy held the door open as Dan followed Clara inside.

The house was old but in good condition. They passed through the large kitchen into the parlor. The sound of a grandfather clock, ticking in steady rhythm, filled the room. Clara guided him that far and bade him take a seat. She disappeared through a rear door, promising to return momentarily. Left alone for the moment, the tall man took in his surroundings. There was a long overstuffed couch with small tables at the end, each bearing a coal-oil lantern with colored glass shades. Two overstuffed chairs of matching material faced the couch. On the walls were small shelves covered with knick-knacks. Next to the grandfather clock was a painting of an old man who looked like he had been inhaling dill-pickle fumes.

The back door of the house slammed and the old gentleman entered, loosening his tie. Dan was still on his feet. "Sit down, young feller," the silver-haired man said, gesturing toward the seating area.

Dan had been holding his hat since entering the house. Laying it on a table, he moved toward one of the overstuffed chairs, spurs jingling. He started to sit down when Clara entered the room, followed by the three offspring. Each found a seat. Dan waited until Clara took her place in the other overstuffed chair, then eased into his own. The old man took a straight-backed chair. The three young ones sat on the couch.

Clara then spoke. "Again, Mr. Colt, I apologize for our behavior."

"Forget it, ma'am," Dan said with a smile. He could feel Molly Jo's stare on him, though his head was turned at a right angle to face Clara.

"I'm Clara Wyler. This is my father-in-law, John Wyler." Dan stood up and shook the old man's hand. "You know Molly Jo's name."

Dan forced himself to meet her stare. She did not smile.

"Randy is our boy." Dan shook Randy's hand, receiving a warm smile in return.

"And this is Dolly." The crippled girl met Dan's eyes with a friendly smile.

"Hello, Dolly," he said, showing his white, even teeth.

As Dan returned to the chair, Clara Wyler said, "My husband, Dolph, was shot down in cold blood by a gunslinger named Ray Pittman, Mr. Colt. Dolph only wore a gun occasionally. Pittman knew it. He got thirsty for blood and deliberately picked a fight with Dolph. My husband told him he was not wearing a gun. Pittman called him a liar and a coward. Dolph pulled open his coat to show that he was unarmed. Pittman drew and cut him down. There were several witnesses. Pittman claimed he thought Dolph was going for his gun." Clara cleared her throat and blinked at the gathering tears. "All the witnesses said Dolph told him he was going to open his coat. He made no fast moves with his hands at all."

"It was murder," John Wyler interjected with a broken voice.

Clara swallowed hard, clearing her throat again. "Your brother saw it and challenged Pittman. Our town marshal was away. There was no one to intervene. Pittman went for his gun and Dave killed him before he could draw."

"I was with him," added the old man. "Never saw a gun leap out of a holster so fast." He eyed Dan's twin Colt .45's. "You as fast as your brother?"

Dan shook his head. "I have no way of knowing. We have not seen each other since we were two . . . at the most, three years old."

The Wyler family listened intently as Dan told them of the day nearly a year ago when he drove the wagon home from Fort Laramie, Wyoming, and found his wife, Mary, brutally murdered. His hired hand was also mortally wounded, but lived long enough to describe three saddle tramps who had robbed and shot them. Dan had met them earlier on the trail—even passed the time of day with them. He left the ranch in the care of close friends and set off to track Mary's killers.

He told of the early days when he made his living as a gunslinger and bounty hunter. He had hung up his guns for Mary's sake. After they were wed in Wichita, he bought a ranch some twenty miles west of Fort Laramie and settled down to a quiet life. It lasted five years.

He tracked the killers to Holbrook, Arizona. There he found two of them. In a cloud of gunsmoke they died on Holbrook's main street. The third one was absent.

Dan told the Wylers of his arrest by Holbrook's town marshal, Logan Tanner. His gunfight with the two killers had been fair, and he was shocked to find the marshal holding a shotgun on him as he turned to leave. The marshal arrested him as one Dave Sundeen, who had resisted arrest and shot the marshal in the process a few months previously.

Molly Jo's countenance began to change slowly as Dan told of his trial and how several eyewitnesses pointed him out as the man who shot the marshal. "Before the trial," Dan said, "Tanner showed me a 'wanted' poster with an artist's sketch of Sundeen. It was *my* face. I knew I didn't have a chance."

Molly Jo asked, "How did you two get separated in the first place?"

"I'm going to explain that right now," Dan continued, setting his blue eyes on the pretty blond girl. A smile tugged at the corners of her mouth. "My parents were traveling in Arizona. I don't even know which direction they were going. I was not more than three. A man named Ben Mason and his wife, Katie, were traveling from California to Texas. They happened upon the dead bodies of my parents. Robbers had killed them and plundered what few possessions were in the wagon. They also found *me*. They took me with them to Texas."

"But what about Dave?" Molly Jo asked, readjusting her sitting position.

"I'm coming to that."

The girl nodded and bent her head forward with interest.

"The Masons gave me a home and raised me. When I was nineteen, two men shot down Ben Mason. I vowed to find them and kill them. In preparing for that, I learned that I had a natural ability with guns."

"Must run in the family," John Wyler interjected. "I never seen nobody move a gun as fast as your brother."

"So you tracked Ben Mason's killers and killed them?" Clara asked.

"Yes'm. In a fair fight," Dan said quickly. "From then on I was a gunslinger until I married Mary."

"Was she pretty?" Molly Jo asked, cocking her head.

"Beautiful beyond mortal description," he answered with a nod.

Clara saw the pain register in his eyes. "Go on with the story, Mr. Colt," she said, flicking Molly Jo a stern look.

Dan knew that they were genuinely interested because Dave had endeared himself to them. He also wondered if hearing his story was relieving some of their own pain by taking their minds off their recent tragedy.

He related to them the grisly moment in the hot courtroom when the judge sentenced him to five years at the Yuma Territorial Prison. He explained that in Yuma Prison he met a convict who had ridden with the gang the day they robbed and killed his parents. Dan was looking straight at Molly Jo when he said, "That convict told me they carried away a little blond-headed boy about three years old."

Molly Jo's eyes dropped to the floor.

"He finally ended up with a family named Sundeen," he said, pronouncing the last word distinctly.

"You don't think he remembers you," Clara asked, shaking her head slowly.

"I didn't remember him," Dan said flatly. "Had a vague recollection of a little blond male playmate, but that's all. I'm sure it's the same with him."

"Mr. Colt?" It was Randy Wyler. "How did you get out of prison?"

"We got a load of bad water delivered to the prison.

Cholera broke out. I was in solitary confinement. Couldn't have any water. Prisoners and guards alike were dropping like poisoned flies. A friendly guard, very sick himself, let me out."

"So now you're after Dave, is that right?" the old man asked.

" 'Bout the size of it," said Dan with a sigh.

Molly Jo's eyes widened. She brushed her hand over her blond hair. "What are you going to do when you find him?"

"Turn him over to the law," Dan answered grimly.

"But he's your brother!" the girl retorted.

"I don't like the idea either, Molly Jo, but the law is breathing down my neck. One of these days they'll catch up with me and I'll go back to Yuma. Only this time they'll throw away the key. The only way I can clear myself is to produce Dave."

Molly Jo's face looked like she had swallowed a mouthful of castor oil. Tears welled in her eyes. "Dave is a good man, Mr. Colt," she said with a sniff. "He is kind and gentle. He—"

The girl was interrupted by the sound of horses approaching the house. Randy darted to the window and parted the curtains. "Four riders, Mom," he said uneasily. "I don't like the looks of 'em."

CHAPTER TWO

Dan stood up and eyed the four base-looking riders over Randy's head. Clara stood beside him. "Do you know them?" Dan asked.

"No. . . . Wait . . . I think I've seen the one with the red hair in town. But he's the only one."

Wheeling, Dan said, "I'll see what they want."

"You wait here," Clara said, extending her arms palms forward. "If I need you, I'll call you." With that, she was through the kitchen and out the door.

Dan followed, stopping at the kitchen window and peering through the curtains.

The riders had dismounted when Clara Wyler met them at the porch. They stood four abreast. The late afternoon sun cast their shadows on the ground in long, grotesque forms. One of them threw a suspicious glance at Dan's black gelding, which stood at the hitchrail.

"Howdy, Mrs. Wyler," said the redhead. "We've come for the money." His face had a red tint, like a perpetual sunburn.

"I beg your pardon," said Clara.

"Don't play dumb, honey," another said. "Jist fetch the money and we'll be on our way."

Dan Colt lifted the twin .45's slightly and eased them back in their holsters. Looking through the door leading into the parlor, he said in a low voice, "All of you stay in the house and get away from the window." He moved to the door, which was partially closed.

"Haven't you got a couple of good-lookin' fair-haired daughters?" another said, his eyes wide.

"You'd only want the oldest one, Cliff," blurted another. "The other one's a cripple. She'd be useless at a barn dance."

All four laughed wickedly.

"Mebbe we'll jist take that oldest one and touch a match to this here place and let it burn," said the red-head. "Unless you fork over that thousand dollars bounty money right now."

Instantly Dan was beside Clara. "The only thing that'll be burning is you in hell, lobster face," Dan rasped heavily. Out of the side of his mouth he said, "Get inside, ma'am. Get away from the door." Clara complied quickly.

The ruddy man's face contorted with anger. "Lookie here, boys," he said with a wicked sneer. "It's the gunnie who plugged Ray Pittman!"

"There's *four* of us, mister," another said in a cold voice.

"So they'll need to dig *four* holes," said Dan, his lips drawn tight.

The red-haired man cursed. "There'll be *four* holes in your belly, big man," he hissed.

"Why don't you kiddies go play in your own yard?" chided Dan Colt, narrowing his eyes. As he spoke, his feet left the eight-inch elevation of the porch and grated softly on the ground. All four looked at the stolid face, the icy, slitted eyes. In unison they stepped back three paces.

The six-foot-three-inch two-hundred-and-ten-pound mountain of manhood said, "Get on your horses and ride."

One of them started to step toward the horses. The ruddy one snapped, "Bob, you hang tight." Bob froze.

"We came for the thousand, big man. We ain't leavin' without it."

"You'll have to cut through me to get it, lobster face," Dan said evenly.

Having faced countless moments like this before, Dan Colt had developed a sixth sense. Most gunfighters never lived long enough to develop it. Dan's hair-trigger reflexes, reacting swiftly and smoothly in conjunction with his ice-water eyes, which seemed to read his adversaries' minds, gave him an edge. He knew the redhead would draw first. The others would follow.

Dan studied the redhead. Unwittingly the man's eyes flashed a signal a split second before his freckled hand started downward. The tall man's right hand moved in an invisible flash. Instead of drawing both guns, his left hand crossed his body and brushed across the hammer too quickly for the eye to see. The Colt .45 was firm against his hip. The gun roared four times, sounding like the rapid fire of a Gatling gun.

Each man received a .45 slug through his heart. Not one had cleared leather, not even the redhead. The foursome lay crumpled and sprawled in a mass of unbathed flesh, lifeless hands still clutching the guns they would never fire again.

Blue smoke lifted skyward from the muzzle as Dan Colt straightened from his crouch and released the cylinder. Punching the empties out and letting them fall to the ground, he slipped four fresh cartridges from his belt and thumbed them into the empty chambers.

He heard the door open behind him and the shuffle of approaching feet. The Wyler family gathered around him in a half circle. Dolly was whimpering. Dan holstered the .45 and put his arm around her. The group stood motionlessly and stared at the inert heap.

John Wyler made a low whistling sound. "I thought I'd seen it all," he breathed, "but I hadn't till just now." Lifting his gaze to Dan's face, he said, "You moved like a well-oiled machine. I didn't know it was possible to fan with such accuracy. How'd you do it?"

"Practice," Dan said quietly, still holding Dolly.

"You always do it that way?" the old man queried.

"Only when there's more than two."

"Oh."

Clara spoke up. "Let's go in the house, children. You've seen enough." Molly Jo and Randy turned and started toward the door. Dolly clung to Dan's arm.

"Mr. Colt," said Clara softly, "it seems that this family owes the Colt twins more than we could ever repay."

Turning Dolly around, Dan said, "You don't owe me anything, Mrs. Wyler."

"But you laid your life on the line just now. If you hadn't—"

"I just did what any man would do, ma'am," Dan interrupted. "I'll take the bodies into town for you if I can use your wagon. We'll let Green River bury them on Boot Hill."

Clara looked toward the western horizon. The sun was setting and the sky was bloodred. "You can do it tomorrow, Mr. Colt. It will be dark soon. You can stay here tonight."

"Oh no, ma'am," he said, "I couldn't—"

"You can stay in the same room Dave slept in," she said, ignoring his plea. "It's a spare room. You will be inconveniencing no one." With that, Clara Wyler moved through the door and into the kitchen. Pausing in the doorway, she looked back. "Hope you don't mind leftovers. With the funeral and all, we girls don't feel like cooking."

After supper the Wylers and Dan Colt sat around

the kitchen table. Dan was nursing a fourth cup of coffee. He looked across the table in the light of the lantern. "Mrs. Wyler, what money were those coyotes after? What did the redhead mean by 'bounty money'?"

"That's partly what I meant when I said we owed a lot to the Colt brothers," Clara said pleasantly. "There was a thousand-dollar bounty on Ray Pittman's head. Your brother collected it and gave it to us."

Noticing that Dan's coffee cup was nearly empty, Dolly stood up and limped to the stove. As she approached with the coffeepot, Dan laid his hand over the cup. "No, thank you, Dolly," he said with a smile.

"I'll take some more," John Wyler said, lifting his cup. Dolly filled it, set the pot on the stove, and shuffled back to her chair.

"Dave knew things would be tough on us with Dolph gone," Clara continued. "He wanted us to have it."

"How did those hardcases find out about it?" Dan asked.

"I don't know," she sighed, "but it wouldn't have been difficult. Dave made no attempt to keep it a secret."

"What are your plans now?" Dan asked with interest.

"Things may change now," Clara said, shaking her head. "Gramps and the children and I haven't had any time to discuss it. It was only two days ago that . . . that . . ." Her throat tightened and tears filled her eyes.

"Was that Pittman who was being buried on Boot Hill today?" Dan asked, trying to get off the tender spot.

Clara nodded, wiping tears with the corner of her apron.

"He'll have fresh company tomorrow," said Gramps, nodding his forehead toward the outside door.

Dan felt the dark blue eyes of Molly Jo studying him closely. Trying to ignore them, he said, "Did Dave tell you where he was going when he left here?"

"No," spoke up Molly Jo. "Only that he had a job to go to down in Arizona."

No one else volunteered any information. Dan assumed that, as usual, Dave had not left a forwarding address. "I think I'll nose around the saloons tomorrow. Dave usually finds himself a poker game. Maybe he told someone where this job is."

Gramps yawned without covering his mouth. Scraping his chair on the floor, he stood up and yawned a second time. "Think I'll hit the hay," he said, walking toward the hallway leading from the kitchen to the bedrooms. "G'night."

The family bid the elderly gentleman good night.

Dolly pushed her chair back. "I'll sleep with you again tonight, Mama," she said tenderly, "since Papa—" Grief overwhelmed her and she burst into tears. Molly Jo took her from the room, fighting tears herself.

Getting to her feet, Clara said, "I'll show you to your room, Mr. Colt." Her face was pinched and tired.

Dan picked up the lantern and followed Clara Wyler down the narrow hallway to the last door. She opened the door and stepped over to a large chest of drawers. On its top was a coal-oil lantern. Striking a match, she lifted the glass chimney and touched the flame to the wick. For a moment the room smelled of burnt powder.

Taking the lantern from Dan's hand, she managed a smile. "Thank you for what you did today."

"Like I said, ma'am," Dan said sheepishly, "any man would have done the same thing."

"Few men *could* have done it, Mr. Colt," she said,

moving toward the door. She put her free hand on the knob and paused. "I must apologize for Molly Jo's behavior. She fell head over heels for your brother. It was nothing he did, really. He spent several days here, helping Dolph paint the place. His nomadic life and rugged manliness overwhelmed her."

"What is she? Nineteen?" Dan asked.

"She'll be twenty next month," Clara nodded.

"He's over thirty," said Dan, slightly amused.

"All she saw was a big, handsome, adventurous he-man." Clara dropped her chin and lifted it again. "Guess I can't hold that against her, can I?"

Dan's curiosity was aroused. "Why did Dave take the time to help your husband here on the place?"

"His horse had thrown a shoe. There's no blacksmith in Green River. They met on the street in town. Dolph told him he had the equipment here in the barn and would forge a new shoe for the gray. We were just starting the paint project. They sort of traded favors."

"I noticed the barn was not finished," the tall man said.

"Dave offered to stay behind and do it, but I knew he had to get on to Arizona. I assured him that we could finish it."

Clara changed hands with the lantern. "I really didn't make myself clear earlier," she said apologetically. "About our plans, I mean. We were painting the place so we could put it up for sale."

Dan's eyebrows arched. "Oh?"

"There is a surgeon in Denver who is working virtual miracles on cases like Dolly's. We took her to a doctor in Grand Junction. He told us of the one in Denver. He sent the results of his examination to Denver. The surgeon wrote back and said he was sure he could help her."

"You were planning to sell the place and move to Denver?"

"Uh-huh. The operation will cost around four thousand dollars. We felt the place would bring just about that amount if it was spruced up."

"But you'd have nowhere to live in Denver without money for a place. What were you going to do?"

"The main thing is Dolly's leg. We decided we'd live in a tent if we had to."

"Ma'am," Dan said, shaking his head, "do you know what the weather is like in Denver in the winter?"

"Well, maybe with this bounty money we can rent something till I can find a way to make a living."

Dan inquired into the nature of Dolly's malady. It was a birth defect. It was getting worse as she grew older. Her limp was becoming more noticeable all the time. As Clara explained the girl's situation, Dan thought of how pretty Dolly was. Every bit as pretty as Molly Jo. What a wonderful thing it would be if her walk could match her face.

Clara bid him good night and closed the door. Sitting down on the bed, Dan was pulling off a boot when he heard a light tap on the door. Boot in hand he limped to the door, still wearing the other one.

Two blond heads awaited him at the door. The girls wore bright-colored cotton robes. Molly Jo held a lantern.

"I thought you little girls had gone to bed," Dan said, towering over them.

"We just came to thank you for what you did today," Molly Jo said, drinking him in with her eyes.

"You could have been killed, Mr. Colt. We'll never forget what you did for us," said Dolly, her face shining in the light.

"I appreciate your appreciation, ladies," said the tall man shyly. "Now you two run along to bed."

"Good night," said Dolly, limping away.

"Dan . . ." said Molly Jo softly.

"Yes'm." Her use of his first name did not go unnoticed.

"You're *almost* as handsome as your brother," she cooed.

"G'night, *young'un*," he said, emphasizing the last word. She tiptoed away and he closed the door.

Dan Colt lay fully awake in the darkness. He thought about Dave Sundeen. He wished things could be different. If only Dave were not an outlaw. What a thrill it would be to find him under proper circumstances and walk unannounced into his life. Even if he had not been arrested and sent to prison for Dave's crimes, they could still meet on good terms.

But it was Dan's grim task to capture Dave and take him to Holbrook, where it had all started. He wondered if Dave could be taken alive. If circumstances forced a shootout, which twin was fastest? Dan questioned whether he could draw on his own brother. Hunching his shoulders in the dark, he thought to himself, *Guess I'll cross that bridge when I come to it.*

He smiled when he thought of Dave helping Dolph Wyler paint his place. Better yet was his giving the bounty to Clara. It was pleasant to know that his identical twin was not all bad.

His thoughts released their hold on present and future things and darted to the past.

The lovely face of Mary settled in his mind. Mary. Beautiful, tender, loving, unselfish Mary. Suddenly he could see her standing in the Wyoming sun, waving to him from the little yard beside the ranch house as he rode in from the range. The sunlight danced on her raven-black hair. Her dark eyes were deep pools, sparkling with fathomless love for her man.

Somewhere in the far reaches of the night, Dan Colt fell asleep, the cold hand of loneliness clutching his heart.

CHAPTER THREE

The morning sun was stretching toward the midway point in the sky when Dan Colt rode the rattling wagon into Green River. Folks were milling about; it was business as usual on what promised to be a mild spring day.

Randy Wyler sat beside Dan, pointing out things of interest. "Marshal's office is up there by the gun shop, Mr. Colt," he said, pointing straight ahead.

Dan noted that there was some kind of commotion going on in the Blackjack Saloon. He figured some drifter was probably drunk already and in need of quieting.

Pulling the wagon to a halt at the marshal's office, Dan noticed a sign in the door window:

> MARSHAL OUT.
> BACK LATER.

Twisting in the seat, he eyed the shapeless forms in the wagon bed lying motionless under a canvas tarp.

"Guess we'll have to wait, Randy," said Dan, perturbed. "We can't keep these bodies out at your place any longer. Got to get them in the ground."

The boy looked at Dan with sadness in his eyes. "Could we go out to the cemetery, Mr. Colt? I mean, since the marshal's not here. Just for a few minutes?"

The tall man studied the youthful face. "Sure. On one condition," he said with a half-smile.

"What's that?"

"That you call me *Dan*."

A smile tugged at the boy's lips. "Sure, *Dan!*"

Green River residents eyed the wagon as it moved toward the south edge of town. The branches of the cottonwoods swayed in the breeze as the two passed through the white picket gate. Randy removed his hat as he followed the path to a fresh mound. Dan stood behind him, his own head bare. The flowers adorning the grave drooped as if they felt the boy's inward anguish.

Randy's shoulders shook as he tried to stifle his sobs. Moving to his side, Dan put a strong arm around him. "Go ahead, boy. Let it out. It's no shame for a man to cry."

The floodgates burst. Dan squeezed tight while Randy Wyler sobbed liberally for several moments. Standing there, Dan read the inscription on the modest grave marker.

As the youth regained his composure, Dan said, "I'll bet you are Randolph Harrison Wyler, *Junior*, aren't you?"

Randy sniffed, running a sleeve past his nose. "Uh-huh."

"Sounds like a mighty fine name to me," said the tall man. "I know you're going to grow up and do it proud."

Randy sniffed again, staring at the marker. He nodded.

"Your dad was forty-three, huh?"

"Yes, sir."

"You can thank the good Lord for one thing, son."

"Hmmm?"

"You got to have him for—how old are you?"

"Fourteen."

"You got to have him for fourteen years. You remember I told you last night how my parents were both killed when I was three?"

Randy sniffed again. "Yes, sir."

"You have something I don't have."

"Hmmm?"

"Memories. I have no memories of my dad. You've got those, don't you, boy?"

"Yes, sir."

"And you've still got your mom. She's a mighty fine lady, Randy."

"She sure is, Dan," the boy said, clearing his throat. A long moment passed. Randy slowly tilted his face toward the man towering at his side. "Thanks, Dan. I'm glad you came along yesterday. We sure needed you. 'Specially *me*."

"You ready to go now?"

Looking into Dan Colt's eyes, Randy said, "Could I just stay here with him while you deliver the bodies?"

"Sure, son," Dan smiled. "Sure. I understand. I'll be back to pick you up shortly."

The boy smiled weakly. "Thanks."

Turning the wagon in a tight circle, Dan eyed Randy kneeling at the fresh mound and drove toward town.

The sign was still in the marshal's window. This time there was an oldtimer sitting in the shade on the boardwalk. Dan climbed out of the wagon and approached the elderly man.

"Good morning, sir," the tall man said cheerfully.

The old man squinted at Dan's face and said nothing.

"You know where the marshal went?"

Cupping a wrinkled hand behind one of his oversize ears, the oldster said with a crackled voice, "Eh?"

Raising his voice considerably, Dan said, "Do you know where the marshal went?"

"No, it's been purty dry," the old man answered.

Shaking his head, Dan said, "The marshal . . . the *marshal*!"

"His office is right there, sonny," he said, pointing a shaky finger.

Dan flashed a look toward the sky and bent low over the wrinkled little man. "Thanks anyway!" he said, nearly shouting.

"It's okay," he said, still squinting.

As Dan walked away, he heard the oldster mumble to himself, "Young whippersnapper must be pert' near blind!"

Turning back toward the wagon, Dan spied a well-dressed man wearing a derby hat coming across the street. Catching his eye, he said, "Sir, who do you see in this town when the marshal's gone?"

Angling toward the tall man wearing the twin Colts, he said, "What do you need? I'm Ed Dunlap, owner of the Utah Hotel and Starlite Saloon."

Dan shook his hand. Recognition lit up in Dunlap's eyes. "You're Mr. Sundeen. Say, I want to tell you I've never seen anyone handle guns like you did with that Pittman fellow. You could have given him a ten-minute head start and still have blown him to kingdom come!"

"Well, I—"

"All you gunhawks know each other, don't you?" Dunlap butted in.

"Only by reputation," Dan said quickly. "Most gunfighters are lone wolves. They seldom get to know each other personally. Why?"

"Do you know Vic Baron?"

Vic Baron. The name struck a solid chord with Dan Colt.

"What about him?" Dan asked, breathing his words slowly.

"Just rode into town this morning. Seems he has

business over at the Blackjack. His kid brother is traveling with him."

Vic Baron. Dan Colt thought back to his early gunslinging days. A picture jumped into his mind and hung there. A dusty Wichita street on a hot, humid day. Baron challenged two of the fastest guns alive and left them dead in the dust. Dan had observed the shootout with awe. The tall, slender Baron was like double-charged lightning.

When Dan met Mary at the height of his gunfighting career, talk was all over Kansas: If Vic Baron and Dan Colt ever squared off, it would be the shootout of the century.

Since Dan had hung up his guns nearly six years ago and taken up ranching in Wyoming, the name of Vic Baron had not once touched his ears. He remembered how men quivered and quaked at the very mention of the man. He wore his guns butts-forward. Voices spoke in hushed tones when men talked of his lightning-swift cross-belly draw. No man had ever challenged him and lived to tell of it.

Suddenly Dunlap's voice broke through Dan's thoughts, ". . . by the look on your face."

Dan blinked his eyes and focused them on the shorter man. "What's that?"

"I said, you *do* know Baron, don't you?"

"Not really," said Dan. "I saw him once. We've never met."

"What was it you wanted with the marshal?" Dunlap asked, casting a glance at the wagon.

"It would be better if I discussed it with him," Dan said guardedly.

"Something of interest in the wagon, I bet," said Dunlap, walking briskly toward the wagon as he spoke.

"It's really not—" Again Dan was interrupted.

"Some forbidden cargo, eh?" Ed Dunlap said as he flipped back the tarp. His eyes swelled in their sockets. Dan positioned himself in order to see the man's face. The owner of the Utah Hotel had a sudden change of complexion. His face went from white to deep red to pale yellow. He held the tarp taut, seemingly unable to move.

Glancing at the corpses, Dan saw that the ruddy-faced gunman's eyes had come open. He recalled having trouble getting them closed. They were staring right at Dunlap's face. Dan took hold of the canvas and worked it from Dunlap's fingers. Covering the corpses once again, he said, "Is there a deputy marshal?"

Dunlap's mouth was hanging open. Slowly he raised his eyes to meet Dan's. "Er . . . ah . . . no. No," he said nervously, "the town can't afford one." Pulling a handkerchief from his hip pocket, he lifted his derby and mopped a sweaty brow. "Please forgive me, Sundeen, but there's something about a dead body . . . I never even attend funerals." Wiping his forehead again, he asked, "Did *you* kill all of them?"

"Yep," Dan said flatly.

"*All at once?*"

"Not exactly," said Dan with a furtive grin. "There was about a fifth of a second between each one."

Dunlap took one final swipe at his brow and donned his derby. "You can take them over to Basil Anderson's," he said, pointing up the street. "He has the furniture shop and the undertaking parlor. He'll end up with them anyway."

Climbing to the wagon seat, Dan thanked Ed Dunlap for the information and clucked to the team. Anderson's place was identified by a faded, weatherworn sign. The combination furniture shop and undertaking parlor was situated directly across the street from the Blackjack Saloon.

Basil Anderson, a short, fat man of fifty, was not overjoyed at the sight of the four corpses. He complained to Dan that the stingy town council paid him too little for the pine boxes. The Boot Hill dead only netted him about five dollars apiece. Anderson did not bother to ask who had killed the four men. His mind was on his financial mistreatment.

Dan helped him unload the bodies and carry them to the back room. The room was spacious. The smell of pine permeated the place. The corpses were laid abreast in a straight line on the floor. Next to a large workbench strewn with wood shavings were four stacks of pine coffins already finished. Dan counted fourteen. On the opposite end of the room lay two factory-made, silk-lined coffins. Eyeing the numerous pine coffins, Dan said, "Anticipating a lot of business?"

"This town seems to be a stopover for crooks, cardsharps, and gunslingers. The Boot Hill crowd seems mighty anxious to meet their Maker. Gotta keep stackin' 'em up so's I don't get caught short." Anderson's voice faded slightly as he left Dan standing in the back room.

Dan turned to follow when he heard the coffinmaker say, "Looks like I'm about to get some more business."

As he made his way toward the front, Dan could hear loud voices coming from across the street. Peering through Anderson's large, dirty window, he could see a crowd gathering as men were jamming the batwings of the Blackjack, trying to get out in a hurry.

Basil Anderson followed Dan Colt through the door and onto the boardwalk. A man was running down the street toward the marshal's office. Another in the gathering crowd was shouting, "Gunfight! Gunfight!"

The eyes of the crowd were fixed on the batwings. From the garbled din of voices Dan's ears picked up the name "Baron" three times.

The noise suddenly fell to a whispered hush as a

youth of no more than twenty elbowed the batwings and stepped into the street. Next, there appeared in the shaded doorway a tall, lean man in his early thirties and with the hard look of an executioner.

Dan Colt's face stiffened. He had not seen Vic Baron since the shootout in Wichita nearly ten years ago. He recognized him instantly: six feet four inches before he slid into his boots; one hundred and eighty pounds of raw, lean meat. His face was thin and leathery, with prominent cheekbones protruding below deep-set steel-gray eyes, cold as marble. His lips were thin and colorless, drawn tight beneath a black pencil-line moustache. His dark sideburns, a scant quarter-inch wide, ran in a straight line from the base of the temple to the square of his jawbone. Strapped to his slender waist and thonged to his thighs were black leather holsters bearing two Colt .45's, butts-forward.

Men talked of him in saloons and around campfires. They spoke with whispered awe of his emotionless appetite for killing, his utter disrespect for human life, and his cold insolence toward death. More than that, they talked of his invisible cross-belly draw.

Baron's black flat-crowned hat shaded his brow as he stepped into the sunlight, his icy eyes scanning the crowd. Behind the formidable gunslick came a younger duplicate of Vic Baron. Then Dan remembered what Ed Dunlap had said: *"His kid brother is traveling with him."* He was dressed exactly like his older brother, even to the pistols holstered with butts forward. Dan could not help grinning. It was almost comical.

Dan recognized in the young man who had preceded Vic Baron the green gunslick stereotype. He had practiced his draw for months. At last, after impressing himself with his speed and accuracy, he had lit out for the nearest saloon to pick a fight. A time or two his lot had fallen on some hot-tempered, callous-fingered saddle tramp who couldn't outdraw a backwoods lumberjack. Now having sent one or two of this type into eternity in a cloud of gunsmoke, he fashions himself a pro. Confidently he sets out to carve his name on the pages of frontier history by challenging one of the big names. By sundown it is carved instead on a crude marker on Boot Hill.

The crowd spread to the sides of the street as the two men squared off, forty feet apart. A man stepped on the boardwalk next to Basil Anderson. "Stupid kid needled Vic Baron into this," he whispered.

From down the street the man who had run for the marshal shouted, "Marshal Ramsey ain't in town!" Baron's brother, standing at the front of the crowd, threw the man a dirty look.

The greenhorn gunslick spread his legs, hunched his shoulders, and positioned his hands like curled talons above his guns. Baring his teeth, he barked, "Make your play, Baron!"

Vic Baron said icily, "You wanted the fight, pee wee. *You* draw."

Dan Colt saw the signal in the kid's eyes. His own muscles jumped in natural reaction. His fists clenched.

Vic Baron deliberately allowed the greenhorn to free his guns of the holsters and start to bring the muzzles to bear before he himself moved his hands.

In less than the twinkling of an eye, Baron's guns roared. One of the kid's guns barked, kicking up dust six feet in front of him. The impact of the forty-five caliber slugs flung the greenhorn on his back. Two holes were in his chest, less than an inch apart, the shirt gathering blood on his pulseless breast.

The crowd seemed frozen in its tracks. Silence prevailed as the lean Baron replaced the shells with live cartridges and adeptly holstered his guns.

The young Baron broke the silence. Stepping toward his brother, he said, "Nobody can say you didn't give him a chance, Vic."

The crowd began to disperse. One of the townsmen walked to the corpse, looked toward Basil Anderson, and said, "Basil! Here's another customer for you."

Anderson grunted something under his breath. Turning to Dan, he said, "Mister, would you mind helping me carry him inside, since you're here?"

Dan Colt nodded and moved into the street toward the body. He noticed the Baron brothers in close conversation with a well-dressed gray-haired man in front of the saloon. Together the three strode to horses tied at the hitchrail, mounted, and rode north out of town.

The rotund Anderson grunted heavily as he hoisted the ankles of the dead man. As they carried him toward the door, Dan asked, "Who's the slick-looking dude that rode off with the Baron brothers?"

Between grunts Anderson said, "That's Spencer Taylor. He owns the Blackjack and the other two saloons on that side of the street, the Birdcage and the Frontier."

While depositing the corpse with the others in the back room, Dan asked Anderson if he knew why the Barons were in Green River. The corpulent undertaker had heard that there was some kind of threat on Spence Taylor's life. Taylor had sent for Vic Baron. The younger Baron had come as a tagalong.

Dan Colt chuckled. "Looks like he's trying to be a duplicate of his brother."

Neither Dan nor Basil Anderson had noticed the entrance of a third party, who was standing in the doorway between the front and back rooms. "So much so, he even changed his name," the man said.

"Oh, good morning, Clete," Anderson said, turning toward the door. Dan cast him a casual glance. "Clete Oliver, this is—" Anderson's face flushed. "I didn't get your handle, stranger," he said to Dan.

"Dave Sundeen," Oliver said before Dan could

speak. Oliver was a plump man whose droopy eyes and heavy jowls reminded Dan of a Saint Bernard.

The tall man started to correct him and quickly decided it was too late to undo the deed.

"He's the gunhawk who took out Ray Pittman," added Oliver.

Anderson rolled his eyes on Dan Colt. "Pittman was a fast man with a gun, Sundeen. You gotta be some slick yourself. I nearly had Pittman nailed in the box before I noticed there were two bullets in his chest. You almost put both slugs in the same hole."

"It's neater that way," Dan said calmly.

Basil Anderson swung his heavy head around, dropping his eyes on the four dead men that Dan had delivered. "Did you—?"

"Yep."

"All at the same time?"

"Yep."

Anderson walked to the lifeless forms, leaned over, and examined each one. He breathed a word neither Colt nor Oliver understood. Standing up straight, he said, "You hit every one of 'em in the same place . . . right smack in the heart."

Dan turned to Clete Oliver. "You said something about the younger Baron changing his name."

Oliver snickered. "Yeah. Boys over at the saloon said his real name is *Henry Otis Baron*." Oliver guffawed. "He wants so bad to be like his brother, he changed his name to *Ric*. Spells it R-I-C!"

"He'd better be as good as Vic," Dan said thoughtfully. "He won't last long if he's not. With that name a lot of young hopefuls will be challenging him."

"Chances are, with experience he'll be as good as Vic," said Clete Oliver, his jowls flopping. "Physiologist back east told me that kind of thing runs in a family."

Dan's thoughts flashed to his outlaw twin. Dave

was smooth and fast with a gun. Apparently Dave had not gained the widespread reputation that Dan had known because he had centered his gunfighting in southwest Texas. It was not until last year that he had begun to travel around the West. Things had gotten too hot for him in Texas. His face had begun to appear on "wanted" posters from El Paso to Fort Worth.

Again Dan felt a wave of dread pass through him. Sooner or later he must pit his skills against his own brother. His identical *twin* brother, the two of them formed in their mother's womb by a rare act of nature. The same haunting thought reverberated through his mind: If he were forced to square off with Dave . . . even if he could outdraw him . . . could he drop the hammer?

CHAPTER FOUR

Dan Colt left Anderson's furniture shop and crossed the street to the Blackjack Saloon. He would start here and, if necessary, work down the street among the other gambling establishments. It was a long shot, but some poker player just might have heard Dave say where he was headed.

As he stepped on the boardwalk, he cast a glance toward the south end of town. He hoped Randy Wyler had not grown weary of waiting.

Pushing through the batwings, Dan paused momentarily, allowing his eyes to adjust to the comparative darkness. The Blackjack was like most saloons he had seen on the frontier. There were the familiar gaming tables, the poker tables, the office at the back, the staircase, and the long bar with the footrail. Brass cuspidors were at each end of the bar; behind it, the long mirror fronted by numerous bottles of rotgut whiskey and glasses turned upside down.

The gunfight had apparently effected a dryness in throats. The place was more active than usual for this time of day.

Dan approached the bar at an empty place between two unshaven cowboys. The bartender—a big, thick-chested man with meaty arms and a bullneck—looked him squarely in the eye and said coldly, "You shouldn't have come back here." His line of sight shifted to something over Dan's shoulder.

Looking in the mirror, Dan saw three men leave a table and move in a straight line toward him. Turning to face them, he leaned back against the bar. The crowd at the bar eased away slowly, leaving Dan standing alone.

The man in the middle had all the earmarks of a cardsharp. The hardcases who flanked him were unmistakably hired guns.

The gambler's features were stiff. His mouth was drawn in a petulant sneer. "You've got more nerve than I gave you credit for," he said through his teeth.

"Yeah?" Dan said, displaying annoyance. "And who might you be?" It was the same familiar situation. Dave Sundeen had an uncanny knack for leaving a bomb with the fuse hissing every time he spurred his horse from a town. Dan seemed to arrive on the scene just as the flame reached the powder.

"You not only got nerve, Sundeen, you're cute too," said the gambler, temper rising. "I want my money."

"I never saw you bef—"

Suddenly the barkeep's meaty arm hooked around Dan's throat, bending his back over the bar. The two gunmen pounced on his arms, flattening them on top of the bar. The gambler's fist made a fleshy popping sound as it found the tall man's jaw. Dan tried to free himself, but the three men had him off balance and pinned tight.

The gambler's eyes were wild as he struck the blond man repeatedly in the face. Dan's hat fell to the floor behind the bar. The man pounded his stomach, causing him to draw his legs upward. Suddenly he realized he could pivot his hips.

The gambler stepped back momentarily to catch his breath. Dan felt a slight relaxing on the part of the men who held his arms. The barkeep was beginning to press against his windpipe.

As the gambler moved in again, fists clenched, Dan lifted the lower part of his body, using the bar as a fulcrum. Doubling his legs back, he straightened them with lightning speed and caught the gambler full in the face with both heels. One spur ripped flesh in the process. The gambler bounced against a table from the impact and slid to the floor like a soggy rag doll. Blood surfaced and flowed freely from a long gash.

In blind anger the man holding Dan's right arm let go and swung a haymaker at his jaw. With the arm loose, Dan had the freedom to reach across his chest and sink his fingers in the other man's eye sockets. He moved so fast that it caught the bartender off guard. Dan's head moved just enough so that the haymaker caught the bartender square on the nose. While the man to his left was howling and stumbling about blindly, the one on his right was trying to regain his balance. In the meantime Dan cupped his hands behind the bartender's thick neck. His own throat was still held loosely in the crook of the big man's arm. The punch on the nose had momentarily stunned him.

With arms like spring steel, Dan Colt swung the bartender heels over head and slammed him hard on the floor, his thick legs colliding with the off-balance man on the way down. The latter was knocked off his feet from the impact.

The hardcase to the left could not see well but was coming at the tall man, both fists flailing. Dan ducked one, bobbed away from another, set himself, and hit the man with a looping right hook. The punch lifted him off his feet and sent him rolling. He came to a stop beneath the batwings, out cold. A pair of dusty boots stepped over him as the batwings spread.

At the precise moment Dan Colt's fist slammed the man, a hammer was thumbed back from the floor behind him.

"*Hold it, Webster!*" a big voice boomed from the direction of the front door. The man on the floor next to the bartender checked himself. He flashed a look toward the thundering voice while pointing the muzzle of his revolver at Dan Colt's spine. The steady muzzle of Marshal Ches Ramsey's Colt .45 was leveled at his head. Cal Webster studied the outline of Ramsey's big frame silhouetted against the doorway.

"Drop it, or they'll bury your body without your head!" Ramsey's voice was heavy and hard. Webster pointed the gun toward the ceiling and released the hammer slowly, then reluctantly laid the gun down.

The bartender was lifting his own thick body off the floor, holding his back. He grimaced with each move.

Marshal Ramsey half-turned and looked at the unconscious man at his heels, then set his sight on the limp, bleeding gambler. After meditating on the hideous gash for a moment, he looked at Cal Webster and the injured barkeep. "Where'd the rest of them go?" he asked, now scanning the quiet crowd.

"Rest of who?" queried the big bartender, gritting his teeth in pain.

A calculated mask of mockery formed on Ches Ramsey's face. "Billy, you're not gonna stand there, look me straight in the eye, and tell me that this one man did all of *this*!"

The bartender slammed a hard look at Dan.

"You been drinkin' too much of your own rotgut, Billy," chided Ramsey. "You're outta shape."

Billy Beck gave the marshal a look of disgust, then fastened his eyes again on Colt. "You'll pay for this, Sundeen," he hissed.

Dan's frosty blue eyes held him severely. "You started it, chum."

"Next time I'll finish it," Beck said thickly.

"You do it, then talk about it, chum," Dan rasped.

Ramsey's voice boomed again. "Webster, you better get one of these men to help you," he said, gesturing toward the crowd. "Parry's gonna bleed to death if you don't get him over to Doc Willis."

Lyle Parry's face was cut in a deep upward slash. It began just below the left cheekbone and cut across the eye socket in a straight line up the forehead. It went about a half-inch into the hairline. There were heavy purple marks forming where Dan Colt's heels had found his face. He was beginning to come around as Cal Webster and another man carried him through the batwings.

Someone had pulled the other man out of the doorway. He, too, was beginning to stir.

As the men were filing out the door, Dan caught a glimpse of Randy Wyler standing outside on the boardwalk, peering through the door. He stepped behind the bar and retrieved his hat. Walking toward the door, Dan rubbed his jaw and moved his chin in a circular fashion, testing its soreness.

Marshal Ramsey was being filled in on the cause of the ruckus by four men who remained for that purpose. He noticed the tall man heading for the door. "Just a minute, Sundeen," he called after him. "I want to talk to you."

"I'll be right outside," Dan said without hesitating.

Ramsey followed on his heels, making some final remark to the four men.

"Hey, Randy," said Dan, putting a hand on the boy's shoulder while still flexing his hurt jaw. "I didn't mean to leave you out there. Ran into a slight diffugilty."

Randy Wyler smiled at the tall man. "That's all right. I just got a little worried that somethin' might have happened to you, so I walked in. Saw the wagon over at Anderson's," he said, pointing across the street. "He told me you were over here."

The marshal spoke from behind. "Mr. Sundeen, I want to shake your hand," he said, extending his own.

Dan turned and gave the lawman a firm grip.

"He's not Dave Sundeen, Marshal Ramsey," Randy said.

Ramsey studied Dan's face with a furrowed brow. "Ain't you the hombre who killed Ray Pittman?"

"No. That was my twin brother."

"Aw, come on—"

"It's true, Marshal," Randy said excitedly. "He come ridin' in yesterday, lookin' for Dave. His name's Dan Colt."

"Now wait a minute—"

"It's a long story, Marshal," Dan interjected. "But it's true. I'm trailing Dave. Important that I catch up to him. The difference in our last names goes back to our childhood."

Ramsey tilted his head and smiled. "Anyway, Mr. Dan Colt, that was some fancy fightin' in there. Lyle Parry and his cronies cause me no end of trouble. I suppose you got in a card game with Parry and he lost."

"No. Apparently my brother took him for a good chunk though. I merely walked in to inquire about Dave and they thought I was him."

"Wow, Dan!" exclaimed Randy, eyes bulging. "I watched you whoop those guys all by yourself! People will think you used an ax on Lyle Parry's face!"

Dan took hold of the brim of Randy's hat and pulled it down over his eyes. The boy pulled it up and said, "Wait'll you see what else he did, Marshal! Four bad men came to our place yesterday, tryin' to rob us of that bounty money Dave Sundeen give us. Dan kilt 'em! *All* of 'em! They're over here at Anderson's."

Ramsey looked toward Anderson's.

"I brought the bodies in this morning," Dan said. "You were out of your office."

The marshal strode toward Basil Anderson's shop. Dan Colt and the boy followed.

They found Basil Anderson in the back room, going through the pockets of the dead men and depositing the contents in a metal box.

"Howdy, Ches," the fat man said, looking up. The body of the greenhorn was separated from the other four by six or eight feet.

Ramsey stood over the four, eyeing the precise location of the bullet holes. Turning to Dan, he said, "How did you manage this?"

"Fanned the hammer," Dan said flatly.

"Ain't nobody can fan that accurately," the marshal said in disbelief.

"They're dead, aren't they?" Dan asked, looking the lawman straight in the eye.

"I don't know how," Ramsey said, shaking his head. "This happened at the Wyler place?"

Dan nodded.

"Right by the house," Randy said excitedly.

"The whole family saw it?"

Dan nodded again.

"All of us," the boy answered.

"Mr. Colt, you just wiped out the Red Thomason gang. They been hangin' around this town for a month, just achin' for trouble."

"They found it," said Dan.

"I think there's a bounty on 'em in Denver," Ramsey said, stepping to the body of the young gunfighter. "I'll check it out. Who's this, Basil?"

"According to some papers in his pocket, his name was Jim House."

"Who did it?" the big man asked, focusing on the two holes in the center of the dead man's chest.

"You ain't heard about this yet?" the rotund undertaker asked with surprise.

"As soon as I hit town, somebody hollered for me to get to the Blackjack."

"You ain't gonna like what I tell you, Ches," Anderson said, his jowls flopping.

Ramsey waited. "Well?"

"Vic Baron."

Dan saw Ramsey's jaw go slack. He swallowed hard and ran a sleeve across his mouth. "*The* Vic Baron?"

Anderson nodded. "The one and only."

Ches Ramsey took a deep breath and let it out slowly through pursed lips. "He must have ridden in last night or this morning," he said, looking at Anderson.

"This morning," the fat man advised.

"Any idea why?"

"Spence Taylor. Talk is that somebody's after Taylor's hide."

"That's no surprise," Ramsey observed dryly. "So Baron is supposed to flush 'em out of the bushes and plant 'em in Boot Hill."

"About the size of it," said the plump Anderson. "He's got his little brother with him."

"Baron has a little brother?" the marshal asked, raising his eyebrows. "Probably serving his apprenticeship."

"And *how*," Anderson said, smiling. "Does his best to look like Vic. I mean all the way. Guns, clothes, hat, boots, stance, posture, walk, sideburns, moustache, and the same cynical sneer. Even changed his name from Henry Otis to *Ric*. Spells it *R-I-C*."

Ramsey lifted his hat and scratched his head. "We got trouble," he mused aloud.

"Well," said Dan Colt, "Randy and I have got to head for home."

"How long you gonna be around?" Ramsey asked Dan.

"Not very. I'll come back into town tonight. Talk to

some other gamblers. Still might pick up something on Dave's destination. Plan to pull out in the morning."

"I'll have to get statements from Clara and old man Wyler," said Ramsey. "Need to do it before you leave. Tell Clara I'll be out a little before sundown."

Dan nodded. "Let's go, partner," he said, putting his arm around Randy. "So long, Mr. Anderson."

As Dan and Randy walked toward the wagon, the two men heard Randy say, "Dan, what's a *diffugilty*?"

The marshal and Basil Anderson stood in the doorway and watched the wagon make a circle in the street and head out of town.

Ramsey wiped a hand over his mouth. "You know, Basil, I think I've got a poster on Dave Sundeen in my office. He's wanted in Arizona. Broke out of Yuma. I never really looked at him close until now."

"You mean you don't believe this 'twin' story?"

"I'm chewin' on it. But one thing's for sure. . . ."

"What's that?"

"I'd sure like to keep him around till Vic Baron leaves. He's probably the only man west of the wide Missouri who would stand a chance with the *Executioner*."

Lyle Parry lay on the examining table in Doctor Sam Willis's office. The stitches in his face smarted like liquid fire. He was cursing the man he thought was Dave Sundeen.

Doc Willis was trying to fit a bandage over the wound. "If you don't quit talking, Mr. Parry, I'll never get you bandaged up."

Cal Webster sat in a chair next to the wall. "Lyle, why don't you relax and let the doc fix your face?"

Parry cursed again. "I ain't gonna relax till that cheatin' skunk is buried in Boot Hill. My face will be scarred the rest of my life. You heard the doc, here. I may never see outta this eye again. Sundeen's gotta die! Do you hear me? He's gotta die!"

It took the doctor several more minutes to place the bandage properly over Lyle Parry's left eye. Parry was breathing heavily, partially from the pain he was experiencing but more from the savage fury burning inside him. He tried to sit up when Doc Willis said he was finished, but the pain stabbed his eye like a red-hot iron. His head felt light and the room seemed to spin around him. He lowered himself flat on the table.

"You'd best lie there for a while, Parry," said Doc Willis. "You've lost a good deal of blood. My advice to you is to head for home as soon as you feel like it . . . and go to bed for a couple of days. I'll drop by and check on you."

"I ain't got time to lay around in bed, Doc," Parry snapped. "There's a man needs killing. I gotta catch him before he leaves town again."

"You'll be in no condition to chase anybody for at least two weeks," the doctor warned. "You'll positively lose that eye if you don't keep off your feet and stay quiet for that long."

The right eye of Lyle Parry bolted a fiery look at the silver-haired physician, then focused on Cal Webster. "Cal," he said with tight lips, "go find Vic Baron."

The task was simpler than Cal Webster had anticipated. He left the fuming Lyle Parry in Doc Willis's office and angled across the dusty street. After belting down a couple shots of Billy Beck's firewater, he stepped out of the Blackjack and into the afternoon sun.

Immediately he saw three horses moving slowly from the north end of town. He recognized Spence Taylor flanked by the Baron brothers. While he waited for the trio to rein in at the hitchrail, he pulled a black wad from his shirt pocket and bit off a chaw.

Spence Taylor read the urgency in Webster's eyes as he pulled the horse to a stop. Looking down from the saddle, he said, "What is it, Cal?"

"I need to talk to Mr. Baron," Webster said, looking straight at the gunslinger.

"Can it wait a few minutes?" Taylor asked, dismounting. "I owe this gentleman for a job well done. Need to pay him and buy him a drink."

"What is it, mister?" the younger Baron asked, stepping to the boardwalk.

"It's not you I'm needin'," Webster said casually, "it's your brother."

Arrogance welled up in Ric Baron's dark eyes. "Anything that concerns my brother concerns me," he snapped, adjusting his gunbelt. His glance bolted Webster hard.

Cal Webster was thirty-nine years in this world. He had killed many a man in a gunfight. His patience wore thin easily. This cocky kid, barely out of diapers, was grating heavily on Webster's thin veneer of control.

"Now what is it that you want?" the youthful Baron asked angrily.

Webster looked at the imperious kid with disgust, then set his eyes on Vic Baron, who stood yet in the street. "Friend of mine is desirous of *your* services, Mr. Baron. He sent me to fetch you."

The older Baron started to speak when Ric stamped a foot hard on the hollow boardwalk and snapped with fury, "When Vic gets hired, *I* get hired!"

Webster, fighting to hold his temper, rolled the tobacco plug to the other side of his mouth and said through clenched teeth, "My friend has a *man's* job in mind, junior—you couldn't handle it."

Ric started to speak again, but Vic said, "Let it go, Ric! I'll talk to the man."

Ric Baron swore. "Ain't nobody gonna talk to me like that!" His face flushed heavily.

"I just did," Webster said calmly and spat a stream of brown juice square in the kid's face. The boy's hands fumbled toward the guns holstered butts-forward on his hips as his eyes blinked against the smarting fluid. Webster sliced a chopping fist to Ric Baron's jaw, flattening him in the street. Both guns fell to the ground.

While the youth rolled dizzily in the dust, Webster said, "Sorry, Mr. Baron, but your little brother is going to have to learn some manners."

"I've told him the same thing," said Vic Baron, eyeing his brother nonchalantly. "His impudence is going to get him killed before he grows up, I'm afraid."

"Who's needing Vic's guns, Cal?" Spence Taylor chimed in.

"Lyle Parry," answered Webster. "That Sundeen gunslick kicked his face in and cut him pretty bad. May lose his left eye. Doc says he'll be laid up for a while."

"Sundeen?" queried Taylor with squinted eyes. "You mean the 'slickie that took out Pittman?"

"Yep."

"I thought he left town."

"He came back."

"What for?"

"I dunno. He walked straight into the Blackjack like he wanted trouble."

Ric Baron was up on one knee, shaking his head.

Taylor spoke to the older Baron. "Why don't you go ahead and talk to Parry? I'll pull the money out of the safe and have it ready for you. We'll have that drink when you come back."

Baron nodded. Taylor headed for the saloon door as Webster angled across the street toward the doctor's office. Following Webster, Vic spoke over his shoulder to his brother. "See you in a few minutes, Ric."

The younger Baron ignored his brother. His eyes were on Cal Webster's back. "Webster, you're a *dead man*," he hissed under his breath.

CHAPTER FIVE

Clara Wyler dusted flour from her hands and walked to the open kitchen door when the sound of the wagon met her ears. She watched Dan Colt pull the team to a halt in front of the partially painted barn. Alighting from the wagon, the tall man unhitched the doubletrees and drove the team inside the corral, the horses happy to be rid of the harnesses. Dan and the boy emerged from the barn and together backed the wagon under the lean-to roof next to the barn.

Dolly, who had been sitting in the shade of the front porch, limped toward them as they approached the house. As Dan watched her coming, his heart became heavy. *Such a lovely girl,* he thought. *There has to be a way to get her to that doctor in Denver.*

"Dolly, wait'll you hear what Dan did!" Randy exclaimed.

"Now Randy," the tall Colt said, "don't blow it out of proportion."

"What'd he do, Randy?" Dolly asked, sliding her hand into the crook of Dan's arm.

"Let's get the whole family together and I'll tell all of you at the same time," said the boy enthusiastically.

The sweet scent of hot bread met Dan's nostrils as the trio approached the kitchen door. Clara met them, smiling warmly.

Dan swallowed the saliva that had instantly gathered in his mouth. Closing his eyes, he drew a deep breath through his nose and said, "That would make a full man hungry!"

While Clara sliced off a large chunk of hot buttered bread and poured him a cup of hot coffee, Randy gathered Gramps and Molly Jo into the kitchen. While Dan sipped the coffee and enjoyed the bread, the boy told of Dan's expert handling of four of Utah's toughest men single-handedly. During the discourse the dark blue eyes of Molly Jo never left the suntanned face of the handsome man.

"Wow, Mr. Colt!" Dolly gasped. "Was it really like Randy said?"

"He added a touch here and there, Dolly," Dan said, smiling. "He also forgot to tell you that I would have a bullet in my back if Marshal Ramsey hadn't come to the rescue."

"Aw, shucks, you'da handled it," Randy said, blushing.

The conversation soon turned to the needs of the Wyler family. Dan announced that he was going to stay long enough to finish painting the barn. Randy and Dolly became emotional, John Wyler happily agreed, Molly Jo smiled with dazzled eyes, and Clara Wyler protested mildly, but soon she also voiced agreement. It was then that the tall man said, "I'll only stay on one condition."

All eyes fastened eagerly on his face. "What's that?" asked Dolly.

"That we quit this 'Mr. Colt' stuff and that you call me *Dan*."

When all had agreed, Dan said, "Now lead me to the equipment. There's still three or four hours of daylight left. We can get a lot of old paint brushed off and be ready to slap new paint in the morning."

* * *

Lyle Parry was still flat on his back when Cal Webster and Vic Baron entered Doc Willis's office. The elderly physician rose from a chair to meet them.

"I brought Mr. Baron, Lyle," Webster said, leaning over the prostrate gambler.

Parry turned his head and set the unbandaged eye on the gunman known throughout the West as the Executioner. Extending his right hand, he said, "I'm Lyle Parry, Mr. Baron."

Vic Baron's stonelike face remained stolid as he gripped the gambler's hand. "You wanted to see me?"

"Got a job for you."

"I'm listening."

"Skunk that did this to me needs killin'." Parry readjusted his head on the pillow, grimacing momentarily. Spreading a sinister grin across his broad mouth, he continued. "You available?"

"Just finished a job. I'm open if the price is right."

"This bird is faster'n average," breathed Parry. "Name's Dave Sundeen."

"Never heard of him," Baron said in a monotone.

"Ever hear of Ray Pittman?"

"Yeah."

"Sundeen took out Pittman in a standoff. Pittman never cleared leather."

"I'm impressed," Baron said with a touch of boredom.

"What's your price?" asked Parry bluntly.

"You wanting this done so's you can watch it . . . or just want it done?" Baron's thumbs were hooked in his gunbelt.

"As public as possible," Parry said through his teeth. "And I want to be there." Squinting the exposed eye, he said, "You don't do it private-like anyway, do you?"

"If you mean a bullet in the back . . . absolutely not. Every man I ever killed was armed and looking at me face to face. Sometimes there's a crowd. Sometimes just the two of us. But always a fair draw."

"I want you to get him right out there in the street, Baron. I want the whole town to see it." Breathing hard, he added, "Mostly I want to see it—for my own enjoyment. Now, how much?"

Vic Baron rubbed his slender chin. Running the tip of his index finger over the pencil-line moustache, he said, "Lately I've been turning my light work over to my little brother. He needs the experience. Mind if I turn it over to him? It'll cost you less . . . and he'll be just as dead."

"You sure he can take Sundeen?" Parry asked skeptically.

"Kid's good," Baron answered flatly. "If it was someone in the Wyatt Earp, Bat Masterson, Hank Blue, Billy Sutton, Dan Colt, or Doc Holiday caliber, I'd handle it myself. Would cost you twenty thousand."

Lyle Parry's eye fluttered.

"Ric'll handle this unknown for you for three thousand."

"But . . . but . . . what if Sundeen should take him?" Parry said nervously.

"I'll be standing by. You have my guarantee. Sundeen won't walk away. He'll be a permanent tenant at Boot Hill. Won't cost you another cent." Baron's voice was frigid.

Parry smiled wickedly. "It's a deal. I'll send Webster, here, to get the money."

"No need," said Baron. "You can pay me when it's done."

"How do you know you can trust me?"

"I don't. But I know where I can *find* you."

Parry stared into Vic Baron's cold, dark eyes and swallowed hard.

"Had a fella welch on me once," Baron said torpidly.

"Yeah?"

"When I went after him, he was wishing he was in hell before he got there."

"How you gonna get him to square off with your brother?" Parry asked with interest.

"Leave that to me," Baron said, turning to look out the window. "Afternoon's moving on. Tomorrow soon enough?"

"Sure," the gambler said, nodding.

"Now, where do I find this Sundeen?"

Cal Webster spoke up. "When he was here before, he stayed with the Wylers, northeast of town. Probably where he is now. I'll give you directions to the Wyler place."

Night came to Green River, wrapping it in a shroud of darkness. An elderly man made his way along the main street, lighting the lanterns that lined the boardwalk. Music rode the cool night air, coming from the saloons. Inside the Blackjack, Vic Baron sat at a card table, playing poker with Cal Webster and two drifters who had ridden into town at sunset. The man at the piano was pounding out a lively tune.

Looking at Baron, who sat opposite him, Webster fanned a new hand. Lowering his gaze to study the cards for a moment, he said idly, "Ric's not joining us tonight?"

Baron had just dealt and was studying his own cards. He seemed engrossed in thought. Slowly Webster's words filtered through. "What's that, Webster?"

"I said, Ric's not joining us tonight?"

"Naw, he's still nursing his jaw where you tapped him."

"You really think he'll be able to handle the man who killed Ray Pittman?"

"Don't rightly know," Baron said, slapping a card on the table. "He's had easy ones right along. It's time he graduated."

"What if Sundeen outdraws him? It'll be too late for you to do anything."

"So he'll be stiff in a Boot Hill grave by this time tomorrow night," Vic Baron said coldly.

One of the drifters, a hardcase named Jack Palmer, angrily threw his cards on the table and said, "I'm out."

Baron's dark eyes settled on him.

"Me too," said Palmer's partner.

Webster dropped his cards to the table and said, "Me too."

Palmer slammed Baron with a hard look as the latter raked in the pot. "You cheated, mister," he snapped. "Dealt yourself a winnin' hand off the bottom!"

Vic Baron's impassionate eyes fixed themselves on the drifter's unshaven face. "I'll give you ten seconds to take that accusation back, cowboy," he said frigidly.

"And if I don't?" Palmer said stiffly.

Baron eyed him with quiet venom. "Then draw."

Cal Webster spoke quickly to Palmer. "Better apologize, cowboy. This is Vic Baron you're talking to."

"I don't care if it's Ulysses S. Grant," the drifter said heatedly. "He's a cheat." As he spoke, Palmer leaped from his chair, clawing for his gun. From under the table a revolver roared. The bullet ripped through the tabletop, scattering splinters and shattering Palmer's belt buckle.

The piano became suddenly silent, as did the entire saloon. Jack Palmer staggered heavily, folded forward, and flopped to the floor. Blue smoke filtered upward through the bullet hole in the table as Vic Baron holstered his gun. The bitter smell of burnt gunpowder hung in the air.

Baron planted his cold eyes on the other drifter. "You think I cheated?"

"No, sir." With that, he donned his hat and moved quickly toward the door.

Ches Ramsey met him at the batwings. "You stay here, mister," barked the marshal. "Nobody leaves this place till I say so!"

It was nearly nine thirty by the time Marshal Ramsey was fully convinced that Palmer had gone for his gun first. As he shouldered his way out through the batwings, the piano struck up a tune.

Spence Taylor approached Vic Baron. "I've got your money and a bottle of imported stuff in the office." Baron nodded his rigid head.

"See you tomorrow," Webster said to Baron.

"Tomorrow," said the Executioner.

Webster waited until Baron and Taylor had disappeared into the office and the door had closed. As he stepped out into the cold night air, he rubbed his arms briskly. Passing under a street lantern, he untied his horse at the hitchrail. He placed his left foot in the stirrup. As he threw his weight to it, orange flame blossomed from a rifle muzzle across the street. As the gun roared, a black hole appeared in the back of Webster's shirt and he fell to the street. His foot hung in the stirrup, twisted.

The frightened horse was preparing to bolt when someone grabbed the reins. Instantly the street was filled with people. "It's Cal Webster!" someone shouted. "Somebody shot him in the back!"

Within two minutes Marshal Ches Ramsey was standing over Cal Webster's body, looking into the shadowed faces of the crowd. "Anybody see anything?" he barked.

Quietly the faces in the crowd eyed each other.

"Guess not, Marshal," an unidentified voice proclaimed.

"One of you boys go get Anderson," Ramsey said, motioning toward Basil Anderson's place of business. The fat undertaker lived in crowded quarters above the furniture shop.

Anderson came on the scene exactly at the same time Vic Baron parted the batwings of the Blackjack. Baron threaded his way through the crowd. His eyes widened as he saw the dead face of Cal Webster in the light of the street lantern.

As Basil Anderson and another man hoisted Webster's body, Baron spoke to Ches Ramsey. "What happened, Marshal?"

In the background the voice of the portly undertaker was heard complaining about the cheap Boot Hill burials.

"Somebody shot him in the back. Rifle." Ramsey shook his head. "I wasn't particularly fond of Webster, but I don't wish this kind of thing on anybody."

Expressionless, Baron turned away and walked down the street toward the Utah Hotel. Passing through the lobby, he mounted the stairs and found his room in the dimly lit hallway. As he turned the key in the lock, he eyed the light shining under Ric's door across the hall. Entering the dark room, he struck a match and lit the lantern on the dresser. He stepped into the hall, tossing his hat on the bed and pulling the door shut behind him.

As he crossed the hall, his eye caught two tall men standing in front of an open door, exposed by the shaft of light coming from within the room. Both men were watching him. Ignoring them, Baron turned the knob of Ric's door. It was locked.

"Who is it?" Ric's voice said from within.

"Vic."

Presently the lock rattled and the door opened.

Without a word the elder brother walked briskly across the room to the Winchester .44 that leaned against the corner. Lifting the chamber to his nose, he sniffed lightly. Instantly Vic Baron's face grew hard. Casting a red eye toward his brother, he said, "You shot Cal Webster in the back."

A sardonic smile crept over Ric's mouth. Closing the door, he said, "He won't spit in my face again."

Vic slammed the rifle in the corner. Scowling angrily, he said, "This is the third time, little brother. I told you before. A backshooter is a coward. I've got more use for a scaly-bellied snake than I do a coward. Now you pack up and hit the trail. You've traveled your last mile with me!"

Defensively Ric whined, "But he spit in my face, Vic!"

"If you wanted him dead, why didn't you wait till morning and choose him out on the street?"

"Well, I—"

"Were you afraid of that two-bit gunhawk?"

"N–no! No, Vic! I just—"

"Clear out, kid. We're through." Vic moved toward the door.

"Wait a minute, Vic!" the younger Baron sputtered, "I promise I'll never do it again!" He was clutching Vic's arm. "The next challenge I'll face 'em in a square draw. I promise." His eyes were pleading.

Vic Baron's face muscles relaxed. "Okay, kid," he said with a sigh, "I'll give you one last chance."

"You're tops, Vic," Ric said with a smile of relief. "I won't let you down."

"You promise me, kid. No more backshooting."

Ric raised his right hand, palm forward. "I swear on Mama's grave,"

"Then sit down. I've got something to tell you."

Ric sank into the only chair in the room. Vic stood over him. "I got you a job today," he said.

"Them four that Dan Colt killed yesterday . . . and the greenhorn and the drifter Vic Baron blew away . . . and . . . and Cal Webster."

"That ain't Dan Colt, Basil," Ramsey said, still focused on the pair about to draw.

"Huh?"

"I didn't let on to him yesterday, but I happen to know that the famous gunfighter, Dan Colt, was bushwacked back in Kansas five, six years ago. Killers dumped him in an unmarked grave."

"Really?"

Ramsey nodded. "This blond dude is Dave Sundeen. He's wanted in Arizona. Broke outta Yuma. He's got somep'n up his sleeve with this cock-and-bull story about bein' his own twin. I gotta arrest him and lock him up. Federal man's on his way."

Ric Baron placed his feet eighteen inches apart. His hands were held at waist level, ready to cross his belly and draw the Colt .45's that rode his slender hips, butts-forward. His face settled into a malevolent gray mask. He was duplicating what he had seen his brother do many times before he cut an opponent down.

Through tight lips, the young Baron said, "Draw, big mouth."

The challenger whipped his gun from its holster and fired. Both of Ric's guns fired at the same instant. Ric felt the bullet rip his loosely-hanging shirt just below the left armpit as the other man fell flat on his back from the impact of both slugs, rolled his head, lifted one knee . . . and died.

Holstering his guns with a flourish, Ric eyed his marble-faced brother. "How was that, Vic?"

The older Baron walked to his brother and examined the torn shirt. "You're gonna have to speed up, little brother. If his shot hadn't gone a mite wild, it would be you there on the street."

"I'll get a little more practice on that Sundeen dude," said Ric with a wide smile.

"That's another one of your problems, kid," Vic observed coldly.

"What's that?"

"You smile too much."

CHAPTER SIX

Dan Colt mounted the crude ladder, paint bucket in hand. The paint-brush handle protruded from the hip pocket of his faded denims, which had belonged to Dolph Wyler. The old shirt he wore had also belonged to the dead man.

Reaching the pinnacle of the roof, he turned momentarily and cast his gaze across the plush valley. The morning sun highlighted the rust red of the canyon walls while broken clouds cast clusters of drifting shadows across the valley. Nomadic breezes pursued one another through the resilient green grass, moving it in ruffling waves. Sparrows argued with chattering squirrels in the cottonwoods that shaded the Wyler ranch.

Randy and Gramps were getting ready to paint the barn doors. Molly Jo sat on a nail keg next to the corral fence, her dark blue eyes fastened on the blond locks of the man on the ladder. The morning breeze toyed with Dan's hair, adding an extra touch of fascination to his already handsome features.

Dolly remained in the house, taking her turn at the breakfast dishes. Clara busied herself in one of the bedrooms.

Dan had hung his gunbelt over one of the fenceposts near where Molly Jo sat. Idly she lifted one of the Colts from its holster. Dan noticed her eyeing it meticulously. "Be careful, Molly Jo," he said with a smile, "that thing is loaded."

Tilting her head, she lifted her gaze toward him and said, "There are no notches on your gun handles. I thought all you gunfighters notched your handles every time you killed a man."

Dipping the brush in the bucket, he said, "Only the egotistical punks do that." Smearing paint over the thirsty wood, he asked, "Did Dave have notches on his guns?"

"I don't know," her voice carried upward. "I never noticed."

As the tall man dipped the brush again, Molly Jo balanced the Colt .45 in one hand and said, "Do you have nightmares about it?"

"About what?"

"When you finally catch up to Dave."

"Molly Jo!" The voice of John Wyler pierced the air. "Why don't you hush up and let Dan tend to his work?"

"She's not bothering me, Gramps," Dan chuckled. Looking at the girl, he said, "Yes, I do. I'm dreading that moment horribly."

"Do you really think you can do it?"

Dan did not answer.

"Capture him, I mean. And turn him over to the law."

"I hope that's the way it will be," said Dan, descending the ladder. As he changed the ladder's position, he said, "I wish it were not this way at all. I wish I could just forget it and give up the chase."

"Why don't you?" asked Molly Jo, the breeze sifting through her own blond hair.

"Can't," Dan said, ascending the ladder. "There's a U.S. marshal by the name of Logan Tanner on my trail. The old bloodhound will not rest till he puts me back in Yuma Prison. If it's not him, it'll be some other lawman. Only way for me to live in peace is to bring Dave in. No other way to clear myself."

The back door of the house opened and closed. Turning to look, Dan saw Dolly step off the porch and slowly limp toward the barn. She smiled warmly and waved. Dan smiled back and waved the paint brush at her.

As Dolly drew closer, Molly Jo stood up, holstered Dan's revolver, and said, "Here, Dolly. You sit on the keg." The older girl climbed the split-rail fence and perched on the top pole.

When Dan had spread the paint as far as he could reach, he once again descended to the ground. John Wyler had partially finished his task on the barn doors and was standing off about twenty yards, admiring his work. Dan set down the bucket and laid the brush on its rim. Joining Wyler, he eyed the paint job.

"This will help the old place to look better, don't you think, Dan?" asked the silver-haired man.

"No question," Dan agreed. Looking down at the oldster, he said, "Are there any prospective buyers for the place, Gramps?"

Wyler shook his tousled head. "Not yet. We're hopin' the sprucin' up we're givin' the old place will catch somebody's eye."

"It's too bad you folks have to give the place up," Dan said gloomily. "This is such a beautiful valley. Mighty nice place to live. Good place to raise these kids too."

"We feel the same way, Dan, but Dolly's leg is more important. We—"

"What I meant, Gramps, was it's too bad there isn't a way to provide Dolly with the surgery and keep the place too."

The old man looked at the ground and shook his head.

"Tell you what, Gramps," Dan said, placing his

hand on Wyler's stooped shoulder, "I've got a little money in the bank back in Texas—"

"Clara would never take it, Dan. None of this family would let you use your savings." Wyler shook his head vigorously. "Nope. We'll sell the place. Dolly will have the surgery. We'll make out. Much obliged, but we'll see it through."

"If you change your mind—"

"We won't, son," said the leather-faced Wyler, "but thanks a whole lot for the offer."

The old man saw Molly Jo lift her head and look off toward the west. Two riders were coming around the house. Dan focused on their faces and eyed his guns hanging on the corral fence.

The Baron brothers paused as they turned off the road and entered the gate of the Dolph Wyler ranch. Their eyes followed the double-rutted wagon trail that threaded its way through the grass and down the gentle slope, ending at the freshly painted buildings. The orderly frame structures were partially obscured by a thick stand of cottonwood trees. The gate was positioned at the crest of the long slope, a little more than half a mile from the house.

"This is the place," Vic Baron said, scanning the surroundings.

"If we veer off a little to the right, we can probably make those first trees down there without being spotted," said Ric, pointing.

Nudging their mounts lightly, they descended the slope and entered the deep shade of the cottonwoods. Dismounting, they ground-reined the horses and crept stealthily through the trees. From a crouching position they found a full view of the back of the house and the front of the barn.

Studying the activity at the front of the barn, Vic said, "That's him, up there on the ladder. Parry said he was tall and very blond. The old man and the kid won't present any problem."

Ric whistled in a muted manner. "Get a load of the blond tootsy by the fence."

"I've told you, kid, women are bad luck. Best you remember that," Vic said sternly.

"Aw, Vic—"

"However, she's our answer."

Ric Baron eyed his brother mindfully. "What do you mean?"

"We'll just take her with us to town and tell him she'll be released when he shows up to face you."

"Hey, that's a good idea, big brother. We'll have his feet to the fire. He'll have to do what we say. I can feel that thousand between my fingers now!"

"Sundeen ain't wearin' no gun," mused Vic as he punched Ric with his elbow. "This'll be—"

"Wait a minute," said Ric hastily. "Look what just came out of the house." His bony finger lined on Dolly as she shuffled toward the barn. They watched her approach Molly Jo and sit down on the nail keg. Molly Jo climbed up and sat on the pole fence.

"Let's take the cripple, Ric," said the older Baron.

"Aw, Vic, come on."

"She'll be easier to handle. Won't be tempted to try and make a run for it."

Ric Baron's face twisted in disagreement. "But Vic, the other one—"

"I said we'll take the crip."

The look in Vic's eyes settled the argument.

"Now let's get going," said the older Baron. As they made their way to the horses, he continued, "I'll put her on my horse with me and you badmouth Sundeen. Put the challenge to him."

Ric nodded as they swung into the saddles.

Rounding the corner of the house at a trot, they saw the old man and Dan Colt standing a short distance from the barn. Their backs were toward the approaching riders. The girl on the fence was the first to spot them. The older man spun around. The tall man followed suit, then looked toward the girls. Before he could move, Vic Baron's grating voice bellowed, "Hold it right there, Sundeen!"

The muzzle of Baron's gun was lined on Dan's chest. His face was twisted in a grotesque appearance. His dark eyes bolted Dan hard. "Make a move, Sundeen, and the whole family dies!"

Ric had both guns drawn, one covering the girls, the other, John Wyler and the boy.

Dan Colt's mind was like a wild beast in a trap, furiously pondering a way out of this outrageous situation.

Vic dismounted and drew his other gun. Holding one on Dan and the other on the old man, he said, "Ric, get the crip and put her on my horse."

As the younger Baron dismounted, Molly Jo regarded Dan's guns looped over the fence post. Vic observed it and snapped, "You, blondie. Get over here by Grandpa." The girl hurriedly slipped off the pole and dolefully made her way to stand beside John Wyler.

Dolly's face was a pallid mask of horror. Ric seized her by the arm and hastened her toward Vic's horse. A feeble cry escaped her lips as the crippled leg gave way and she fell to the ground. The brutal gunslick jerked Dolly to her feet savagely.

Rage ignited in Dan Colt's veins, turning his blood to molten lava. Impulsively his body jerked. Instantly Vic Baron's left-hand gun roared, sending a bullet between the heads of the old man and Randy Wyler. It struck one of the heavy metal hinges on the barn door and caromed away with a shrill whine.

Dan checked himself. The fury within him was causing him to breathe heavily.

"Put her in the saddle," Vic commanded without turning his head.

As Ric hoisted the terrified girl upward, a sharp feminine voice from behind struck Vic Baron's ears.

"Drop those guns!"

Turning his head but still holding the guns steady, he saw the florid face of Clara Wyler behind a Winchester .44.

"Drop 'em!" she bellowed.

Having completed his task, Ric stood beside the horse, his hands poised in front of his belt buckle. His eyes were on his brother.

In a cold, calculated manner the elder Baron said, "You will notice, lady, that both my hammers are cocked. These guns have hair triggers. If you shoot me, they'll both fire. The old man and your big boyfriend, here, will both get it."

Clara observed but did not speak. The silence spoke for itself.

"Now you just put down that rifle and come around here."

Vic Baron's admonition left Clara with no choice. She eased the Winchester down and let it flop to the ground. Slowly she circled the nefarious gunman and took her place behind her son.

"What's going on here?" Dan said heatedly. His glance darted to Dolly astride the horse and back to the tall, sinister man holding the guns.

Vic flashed a quick look to his younger brother. Promptly Ric Baron strode to stand facing Dan Colt. Slitting his dark eyes, he said, "I'm calling your hand, Sundeen."

"What's the girl got to do with it?" Dan rasped, nodding his head toward Dolly.

"Quit asking questions, you yellow-bellied sidewinder!" The kid's face was contorted like the bark on an old oak tree. "You afraid to draw against me?"

Dan turned and fixed his ice-blue eyes on Vic Baron. "What is this, Baron? Who put the burr in this punk's long handles?"

Vic Baron's eyes widened. "You know me, eh? We meet somewhere?"

"Not formally. I saw you gun a couple fellas in Wichita once."

"Kid's doing my light work these days. He wants a shootout. You gonna oblige him?"

Dan's jaw squared. "Gladly. My guns are right over—"

"Not here!" snapped Ric. "You and me are gonna square off on the main street in Green River. We're taking the crip, here, as insurance that you'll show up."

"Don't need to do that," Dan said levelly. "I'll go with you right now."

"Uh-uh," said Ric. "You would be a bellyful of trouble on a ride into town. You wait thirty minutes after we ride out. Then you sashay into town. I'll be at the Blackjack. I want you to come in and badmouth me in front of the crowd. Then challenge me. I'll gladly accept and we'll step out on the street. You understand?"

Dan looked again at Vic. "When I kill your brother, what are you gonna do with the girl?"

Ric Baron ejected a belly laugh.

"Your chance is as slim as a snowball—"

Dan sliced in on Vic's words. "*What about the girl?*" he demanded angrily.

"I don't hurt women, Sundeen. The Executioner never hurt a woman. Of course, if you balk, I'll be forced to."

"After I lead-gut him, it's you and me?" Dan's eyes held Vic Baron hard.

"*If* you do it, yes. But it'll be face on and fair. I don't shoot men in the back. I'll have the girl where you can't see us, but I can see you." Baron lifted his shoulders, moved them in a circular fashion, and said, "You have my word, Sundeen. The minute you and Ric step into the street, I'll turn her loose. But the family has to stay here. Got it?"

Dan spoke to Dolly, who sat trembling in the saddle. "When he lets you go, you beeline for the marshal, Dolly. He will probably be right there on the scene. If not, and he's not in his office, you go to one of the shops where there's a woman and tell her you need to stay there. When I'm through with these two, I'll find you and bring you home."

Dolly nodded, her face ashen. Ric Baron laughed again.

"Put your guns on them, Ric," said Vic, "while I mount up." Holstering his guns after his brother had complied, Vic was behind the saddle in one smooth leap. Drawing one revolver, he placed the muzzle at the base of Dolly's skull. With the other hand he reached around her and lifted the reins from the pommel. "Let's go, little brother."

Ric was quickly in the saddle. Casting a callous glare at the tall blond man, he said, "See you in town, yellow belly."

Dan Colt's fingers flexed impatiently as the Baron brothers rode out of the yard. Vic's gun was still pointed at Dolly's head. John Wyler held Clara tightly. Molly Jo rushed to Dan Colt's side. Without taking his eyes off the two horses, he curled a strong arm around the girl's shoulders.

Slowly the huddling group walked toward the wagon trail in order to see past the trees and keep the receding riders in view. They watched quietly until the Baron brothers and Dolly Wyler crested the hill at the gate. For a brief moment they were silhouetted against the western sky. Then they were gone.

Clara Wyler spoke first. "Dan, who are those slimy snakes?"

"Vic Baron is a first-class gunslinger, Clara," Dan answered softly. "He's known as the Executioner. Prides himself on wearing his guns backward and yet being known as one of the fastest men alive. Some men kill to live. He lives to kill."

Molly Jo's fingernails bit into Dan's muscular arm. "Oh Dan, what are you going to do?"

"Only one thing I *can* do. I've got to kill both of them," the tall man said grimly. "The kid will be no problem. Vic . . . well, he's something else."

Molly Jo ejected a mournful whimper.

"What's behind it, Dan?" asked John Wyler.

"At first I thought it was something my brother had done to them, but I don't think so. Looks like the kid might have learned about Dave outgunning Ray Pittman. Pittman was well known as a fast gun. The way to make a reputation in a hurry is to outdraw and kill a man who just outdrew and killed a fast gun. His wanting it public-like makes me think young Baron wants to climb a notch closer to his brother."

"A blind man could see that the punk is trying to fit into the big brother's mold," said the old man. "If his brother ever develops an ingrown toenail, the kid will probably want one too!"

"Will he keep his word about Dolly, Dan?" Clara asked worriedly.

"Yes. You needn't fret about that. It's a strange thing, but the most vile, corrupt gunslinger has an odd fixation about his word of honor. 'Code of the West,' they call it. As long as I show up, no harm will come to Dolly."

Clara tilted her face upward, looking the tall man straight in the eye. "Tell me honestly, Dan Colt. What are your chances against this Executioner?"

Dan cleared his throat. Randy stood motionlessly,

his eyes fixed on Dan's tanned, angular face. The others waited.

"Well, Clara, that's a tough question to answer. A man can't know that sometimes. By that I mean that I know I can take the kid because I've been at this gunslinging business for a long time. He's green, clumsy. But Vic . . . he's seasoned and extremely fast. In addition to that, he's known to have an unearthly contempt for death. Stories about him tell how he has faced the grim reaper under impossible odds and walked away the victor. In fact, that's his name: Victor."

The last thought hung in the air for a quiet moment.

"Then what you're saying," Clara said, breaking the silence, "is that there is no way to know who's fastest till you shoot it out?"

"Mmm-hmm. That's about the size of it."

Molly Jo began to weep.

"Now Molly Jo, don't you start that. I've lost count of how many men I've drawn against, but there've been a lot of famous ones in the pack. I'm still here."

The girl buried her face in Dan's paint-speckled shirt and sobbed for several minutes. Patiently her mother took the girl's hand and said, "Come on, honey. Dan's got to change his clothes. He'll need to be riding in a few minutes."

Exactly thirty minutes from the time the Baron brothers had ridden away with Dolly, Dan Colt thonged down his holsters and deftly slipped out the twin .45's, checking the loads. The four Wylers clustered close to him.

"You'll be back, Dan. I just know it," said the boy, faking a cheerful tone.

"Sure he will, Randy," said Gramps, patting the boy's shoulder.

Clara looked at him through misty eyes. "We'll be watching for you and Dolly to come down that hill."

Dan nodded. As he turned toward the big black gelding, Molly Jo suddenly ran to him, reached up, pulled his face down, and kissed him on the lips. She clung for a brief moment, then let go.

"See you later, little lady," the tall man said placidly.

Swinging into the saddle, he smiled and rode away.

The four Wylers followed him toward the edge of the yard, halting where the double-rutted wagon trail bit into the grass. They watched quietly until Dan Colt crested the hill at the gate. For a brief moment the broad-shouldered man was silhouetted against the western sky. Then he was gone.

About midway between the Wyler ranch and Bluff City, the Baron brothers topped a rise in the road. Immediately their eyes fell on the lone rider who was coming toward them from the bottom of a shallow draw.

Ric Baron cursed. "It's that stupid town marshal. Now what do we do?"

"Too late for dodging him. He's seen us," said Vic. Putting his mouth close to Dolly's ear till she could feel the warmth of his breath, he said, "If you don't want to see the lawman die, honey, you play along. Your grandpa was a friend of our dad's, see? We dropped in for a friendly visit. You needed a ride into town to . . . ah . . . to get fitted for a new dress. Got it?"

"Yes," said Dolly faintly.

"Your grandpa's coming after you later. Got it?"

"Yes."

"Now put on a happy smile."

As the Barons drew abreast of Ches Ramsey, they smiled thinly and pulled rein. Halting his horse, Ramsey looked at the girl and said, "Hello, Dolly." There was a note of suspicion in his eyes.

"Good morning, Marshal Ramsey," Dolly chirped. "These nice men are giving me a ride into town."

The seasoned lawman maintained his guarded expression. Locating Vic Baron's eyes with his own, he said, "What were you two doing at the Wyler place?"

"Dolly's grandpa is an old friend of our departed father, Marshal," said Vic seriously. "We thought we'd pay him a visit. Our old daddy used to talk so much about his old buddy. They used to ride trail together."

"Yeah?"

"Mmm-hmm. Ain't that right, Ric?"

"Sure enough, Marshal," answered the slender youth. "We thought it would be neighborly if we was to stop in, since we were right near."

"Your father told you a lot about old *Clarence* Wyler, eh?" queried Ramsey.

"Yessir, he and old Clarence used to have mighty big times," laughed Vic, hollowly.

Dolly's heart was in her throat. She knew what Ramsey was doing.

The marshal's leathered brow furrowed. His eyes seemed to lose their color. "Wyler's name is not Clarence," he said through his teeth. His hand dropped toward his gun as he added, "It's *John*."

Before Ramsey's hand closed on the handle, Vic had palmed the gun on his left hip with his left hand. The dexterity of his draw was astounding to Ramsey, whose jaw hung loose.

"You're too clever for your own good, Ches," snarled Vic Baron.

Eyeing the dark muzzle, Ramsey said, "What's going on?"

"We got a little shootout gonna take place in your town," rasped Ric. "We don't want you messin' it up."

Holding his gaze on the marshal, he said, "What we gonna do with him, Vic?"

The elder Baron's eyes were fixed on Ramsey's face. "I guess we could kill him, but killing lawjacks gets sticky. Let's just put him out of commission until you gun down Sundeen."

The marshal's face stiffened. "He's a wanted man, Baron. I'm heading for Wyler's to pick him up now. There's a federal man on the way to return him to Yuma. You're gonna bite off more than you can chew. You talk about sticky—"

"Shut up, Ches," Vic said saucily. "My brother's gonna plug the blond wonder in about forty-five minutes. If your federal man isn't here by then, he'll just be too late. *Get off the horse.*"

As Ramsey dismounted reluctantly, Vic Baron slid over his horse's rump to the ground. "You watch the girl," Vic said to Ric. "I'll be back in a minute."

Baron steadied his gun on Ches Ramsey. Reaching down, he lifted the lawman's revolver and tossed it into a thick clump of grass. There was a deep arroyo off the road about thirty yards, lined with spruce trees and heavy bushes. The gunman herded Ramsey to the low side of the trees, where he could not be seen from the road. Motioning toward a thin-trunked spruce, he said, "Give me your cuffs and sit down."

Sullenly Ramsey lifted the handcuffs from the back of his belt and handed them to the stone-faced Baron. Knowing what the man wanted, he sat on the ground, straddling the tree. Quietly he wrapped his arms around it.

Baron leaned over and snapped the cuffs on his wrists. Standing to full height, he said, "When you wake up, Ches, you can start hollering. Somebody will hear you from the road."

"When I *what?*"

Baron's gun barrel came down hard, crushing the Stetson and smiting Ramsey's head with a dull meaty sound. The lawman slumped limply against the tree.

Once again on the road the Barons soon found themselves riding past the somber, windswept Boot Hill. A quick glance revealed seven open graves sided by mounds of freshly dug earth. Almost immediately they sighted a wide wagon coming toward them, bearing seven pine boxes lined crosswise in the bed. The rotund Basil Anderson sat on the seat, holding the reins. Three men sat on the crude coffins.

Curiosity eating at his insides, Vic Baron lifted his hand, signaling the wagon to stop. Anderson pulled on the reins. As the horses met the wagon, the Bluff City undertaker said, "Howdy, Miss Dolly."

The girl managed a smile. "Good morning, Mr. Anderson."

"Some kind of a big shootout?" Vic asked, scanning the wagon bed.

"Well," said Anderson with a note of exasperation, "you killed two of them. That hotshot kid and the drifter, Palmer. Another one is Cal Webster. Somebody shot him in the back."

Ric Baron felt his brother look at him from the corner of his eye.

"These other four," continued the fat man, "went down in a shootout with that Dave Sundeen hawk."

The younger Baron's face lined heavily. "You don't mean *all at once*."

"All at once," echoed Anderson.

"*He* told you this?" queried Vic.

"Yes, sir."

Vic snarled and spat. "He probably bushwacked them and fed you a fancy story."

Dolly Wyler turned her head to address the man mounted behind her. "He shot them all at once. I saw it. It was at our place."

"Girl's telling the truth," said Anderson. "All four of them were armed and facing him. Each one has a bullet straight through his heart."

Ric Baron's face darkened, then turned a chalky white. His mouth took on a cottony texture.

"We're keeping these men from their work, Ric," said Vic advisedly. Touching his horse's sides, he said, "See you later, gentlemen."

When the wagon was out of hearing distance, Ric said, "Vic, if he took those four—"

"Forget it, kid. Something's fishy."

"I *saw* it," Dolly insisted, raising her voice.

"Vic—"

"He got lucky, kid."

"But Vic—"

"Okay, Ric. I'll take him . . . *and* the thousand."

Ric Baron said nothing until they were dismounting in front of the Blackjack Saloon. "Vic, if he could take all four of those—"

"I said I'd do it," Vic said disgustedly. "I'm going to take the girl to my hotel room and tie her up. You go get yourself a drink. I'll be back by the time Sundeen gets here."

Ric Baron spun on his heels, a touch of shame burning his face. Vic walked away, Dolly limping at his side.

Ric shoved himself through the batwings. As his eyes adjusted to the relative darkness, a sharp pang of terror shot through his heart and spilled icewater into his veins. Before him, leaning on the bar, was the tall blond man.

The young gunslick swallowed hard. "How—"

"You fellas ride awfully slow," Dan said in a subdued voice, "I caught up with you when you were talking to the men with the wagonload of coffins. Made a circle around you. Didn't want to be late."

Ric Baron's insides were churning.

Raising his voice above the din of voices in the saloon, Dan said, "Oh yeah? You think you can, huh?"

Ric blinked his eyes. His body went rigid, fear making his knees feel weak as water. Suddenly he felt Dan's palm sting his face.

Every eye in the place was fixed on the two men. The bullnecked Billy Beck lurked behind the bar, glaring at Dan Colt.

Dan slapped Ric again. "I'm calling you, punk!" Colt's voice bit the air. Ric Baron was on the spot. The tall man was fulfilling Ric's own directive. His reputation as a cold, tough, fearless gunfighter was at stake. He must see it through. Even if Vic showed up now, it was too late. Too many witnesses were watching. He must accept the man's challenge. He summoned every ounce of reserve strength. "Let's go," he said, touching his stinging cheek.

The crowd followed.

At the Utah Hotel, Vic Baron finished tying Dolly Wyler to the metal bed. Fashioning a gag out of a torn strip of pillowcase, he leaned over to place it on her mouth.

"There's something I should tell you, Mr. Baron," she said hastily.

"Yeah? What's that?"

"You're planning to shoot it out with the wrong man."

"What do you mean?"

"Dave Sundeen left town four days ago. The man you're going to face is *Dan Colt*."

Baron's jaw slackened. The name seeped its bitter way into his brain. *Dan Colt!* The only man anyone on the western frontier had ever dared to compare to Vic Baron. *Dan Colt!* Baron's secret, shadowed nemesis. *Dan Colt!* Lightning on wheels.

"Dan Colt was bushwacked and buried five years ago," Vic said, trying to reassure himself.

"No, Mr. Baron. The man who killed those four men at our place is Dan Colt."

Sweat formed on Baron's brow. The description he had often heard of the feared Dan Colt filtered through his mind. It fit the tall blond man perfectly.

"There's no use keeping you here," said Baron, untying the crippled girl.

Wheeling he rushed through the door and bounded down the stairs. As he stepped into the late morning sunshine, his eyes focused on Dan Colt and Ric Baron. They were facing each other in the middle of the street, feet spread, hands poised.

CHAPTER SEVEN

Four hundred and fifty miles south of Green River, Utah, Otis Becker scratched his beard and took a deep puff from his cigarette. A broad grin spread across his face, exposing a mouthful of yellow teeth. In the palm of his hand lay a gold pocket watch taken from some passenger on a stagecoach he had robbed three weeks earlier.

"Eleven o'clock," he said aloud to himself. "Right on time."

Becker squinted his eyes against the Arizona sun, fixing his gaze on the three dark shapes outlined against the crest of the long hill on the southern horizon. Apparently the boss had found it necessary to remain in Tombstone.

The unshaven, hulking Otis Becker had hoped the boss would be able to come along. He wanted him to see this old ranch house for himself. It made a perfect hideout. It was situated among a stand of mesquite trees in a low area, about a mile off the road between Oracle Junction and Tombstone. The barn and outbuildings had burned to the ground some years gone by.

The house was adobe with a low sod roof. Becker had chanced upon it when he was caught in a sandstorm a few days earlier. Having lost his bearings on the road, he stumbled upon it by accident. Moving inside the well-preserved house, he took refuge from the storm. In one bedroom he found the skeleton of a man lying in a disjointed manner on the rusty springs of a bed. Discolored fragments of mattress surrounded the bones. The rotting flesh had decayed the bedding and the portions of the mattress that touched it.

Apparently the man had lived and died alone. No one knew or at least cared about his lonely existence. There was no one to provide even a decent burial.

This old house would prove to be a perfect place for the gang to hole up in after each bank was robbed. Becker had counted on the boss coming with the boys this time, so his first ride out here wouldn't be at night. It would be more difficult to find in the dark.

Presently the three shapes took form. Becker leaned against the remains of the corral fence, blowing smoke toward the brassy sky. He used up one cigarette and had time to build and smoke another before the three unwashed, hard-featured men rode into the yard. Dismounting to the sound of creaking leather, they tied their horses to the leaning hitchrail next to Becker's mount.

The first to speak was Mack Evans. He was a heavy-set man, similar to Otis Becker only much bigger. His dark face was well hidden behind a heavy gray beard, which matched the thick shock of prematurely gray hair bulking over his soiled collar. "You've done yourself proud, Otis," said Evans. "The boss will like this. How's the shack on the inside?"

"Good shape, Mack," Becker assured him in a gravelly voice. "I shucked the bones and the old bed in a hole out behind the ruins of the barn. Found a broom and tidied the place up some. Well-water was brown and brackish for a while, but it's purty good now."

The second man to speak was Neal Furman. His dark eyes were set deep below a portruding forehead.

Coal-black hair dangled from beneath his filthy flat-crowned hat, making his ears invisible and brushing against his foul beard. "This place is next to nowhere, Otis. I like it. House is built solid, like a fort. We could hold off a posse from in there if we had to. Couldn't burn us out. Roof is sod." He scratched under his arm. "Yep. I like it."

"Let's hope we don't have to hold off no posse," Becker said, shaking his head. "Let's hope we can shake 'em each time and leave 'em runnin' in circles while we hole up here, safe."

Dick Millard, the third man, was reticent. Without a word he walked about the place, looking off in all four directions.

Tossing a glance toward him, Otis Becker said, "What about it, Dick?"

Millard, by far the youngest of the repulsive four, turned his cold green eyes on the hulky Becker. His thin face showed no emotion. "You gentlemen are older and more experienced than Dick Millard," he said evenly. "If you say it's good, it's good." Lifting his gaze toward the sun, he said, "Bank in Oracle Junction is seventeen miles from here. Otis, you said it closes at two o'clock. We'd better get moving."

"Right," answered Becker, scratching his beard. "You boys take your bedrolls into the house and find yourselves a sleeping place. Mine's already marked off where you'll see my bedroll."

Untying their bedrolls from the saddles, Evans, Furman, and the tall, gangly Millard carried them inside the adobe house. Otis Becker followed along. "I was hoping the boss would be able to come with you," he said to no one in particular.

"Somethin' came up," said Mack Evans. "He couldn't leave the office. Said he'd ride out tonight. Probably near midnight."

"Place'll be harder to find in the dark," said Becker.

"He's got your map. He'll find it all right," Evans answered confidently.

As Dick Millard laid his bedroll down in a far corner, a lizard zig-zagged swiftly across the floor. The slender outlaw drew his gun and fired, missing the lizard. The little reptile dove through a crack in the floor and disappeared.

Neal Furman guffawed. "Gotta be faster'n that, kid, if you're gonna make a gunfighter."

Millard broke the action and punched out the spent shell. Replacing it with a fresh one from his gunbelt, he dropped the gun in its holster.

"Don't you worry none," chided the burly Evans. "When that Dave Sundeen gets here, he'll show you how to draw and shoot. The boss says he's like accelerated lightning."

As the foursome exited the house, Dick Millard said, "Mack, where'd the boss run on to this Sundeen?"

"He's never seen him, himself," said Evans as each man listened intently. "Friend of his named Eddie Dalton knew this Sundeen over in El Paso. Told the boss about his twin Colts and speedy hands. Boss thought he'd be a big asset for the Tucson job. As you well know, that one could get sticky. Sundeen's not only fast, he's dead accurate, and according to the boss's friend, he has nerves of steel."

As they mounted up, the others agreed that if Dave Sundeen was all he was cracked up to be, he would be desirable for the Tucson job.

"You got the bag, Mack?" Becker asked the formidable Evans.

The canvas bag was hanging by a leather strap over the pommel of Evans's saddle, on the opposite side of the horse. Patting the bag affectionately, he said, "Yup. Right here." From the pommel of each saddle hung a tightly wrapped bundle of burlap. Looking each horse over carefully, Evans said, "I guess we've all got our burlap sacks."

"How'd the boss get in touch with Sundeen, Mack?" asked Neal Furman.

"Boss's friend was meetin' with Sundeen up in Colorado. Said he'd tell him about the Tucson job. The friend said he had no doubt that Sundeen would come. Not with that big payload waitin'."

Furman's brow furrowed. "Is the boss gonna let him know—"

"Nope," answered Evans briskly. "Not till he's had a chance to meet him and observe him for a while. Boss's friend says he's all right, but he wants to make dead positive before he reveals the whole setup. He's supposed to ask for me at the Capitol Saloon in Tombstone. Bert Riley will let me know when he shows up. I'll bring him out here. When the boss is satisfied he's okay, the boss'll come and meet him here."

The outlaws spurred their mounts simultaneously and headed north.

Gusts of wind whipped around the four riders, flopping their hat brims and sending clouds of dust across their path as they rode into Oracle Junction.

The main street was lined with high-front buildings, most of which were in need of a fresh coat of paint. The town was five blocks in length. The First Bank of Oracle Junction was situated in the middle block, on the southwest corner. It was the only stone building in town.

The four riders rode past the bank and reined in at the hitchrail in front of the general store next door. Otis Becker pulled the stolen watch from his vest pocket.

"Twenty minutes to two," said the large man. "Let's let some of them people clear out before we go in.

Why don't we mosey into the store, here, and kill a few minutes?"

At one fifty-eight Mack Evans exited the general store alone and propelled his big frame through the front door of the bank. As he stepped inside, he lifted the neckerchief over his nose. His hat was pulled low.

An elderly man was the only customer. He was just turning from the teller's cage when he glimpsed Evans's masked face. His line of sight fell to the gun in the man's right hand. A stifled cry escaped his lips.

Immediately the teller looked up. He was a small man in his midfifties. His eyes widened.

Evans whipped his left arm around the elderly customer's neck and put the muzzle of the revolver to his head.

"You!" Evans barked to the teller. "Come out here! There'll be three other men coming to the door, one at a time. You let 'em in, savvy? When the last one comes, you lock the door and pull the shade."

Behind the teller a portly woman spun around and gasped. She opened her mouth to scream.

"You holler, lady, and I'll smear grandpa's brains all over your bank! And yours'll be next!"

The bookkeeper clamped a hand over her mouth, fear lining her face.

"Hurry it up!" shouted the scurrilous Evans to the frightened teller. The thin little man quickened his pace, pushing past the waist-high swinging gate.

Dick Millard was already at the door, face masked. The teller opened it and swung it shut behind him.

"Get back there and tie fatty up," Evans said to Millard. Turning to the teller, he said, "Is the hotshot back there in his office?"

"N–no, sir," stammered the teller. "He went home early. He wasn't feeling well."

"He'll be a lot sicker real soon, won't he?" said Evans with a chuckle.

Neal Furman was next. His bushy black eyebrows seemed heavier with the lower part of his face covered.

"Check the back office," ordered Mack Evans. "Make sure nobody's in there."

Furman disappeared into the office and the thick-bodied Otis Becker came through the front door, a large canvas bag folded under his arm. The teller turned the key and lowered the shade.

"I'm sendin' the old gent back there," Evans called to Dick Millard. "Tie him up too. Gag 'em both."

The old man, glad to be free of the big outlaw's sinewy arm, quickly shuffled through the gate and made his way behind the cage. Furman returned, announcing that the office was empty. Otis Becker stayed by the door.

Directing his attention to the teller, Mack Evans said, "All right, let's get it."

Within a minute the slightly built teller had emptied the cash drawer in his cage. Evans and Neal Furman followed him to a back room, where they removed several bundles of bills from the safe.

"Now the big stuff," Evans said to the small man.

The teller shrugged his shoulders. "That's all there is."

Mack Evans's eyes grew dark and virulent. "I know better, runt," he snapped. "Where is it?"

"I said that's all there—"

The big man's heavy hand came across the teller's face with an open-handed, stinging blow. His knees buckled, but he kept his balance.

"I know about the cash shipment from Santa Fe. I know a decoy is riding the Fargo Stage to San Diego. I also know it is being kept here to be smuggled on to San Diego later."

The teller's face blanched.

Evans pointed his revolver between the teller's widened eyes and thumbed back the hammer. "Now is that hundred thousand worth dyin' for?"

Swallowing hard, the little man said, "There's a safe in the floor of Mr. Simpson's office."

While the outlaws emptied the safe in the president's office, the teller asked Mack Evans, "How did you know about this?"

"Our boss has connections," Evans answered flatly.

Leaving the teller bound and gagged with the others, the four robbers left the bank one at a time. Slowly each man mounted his horse and headed south.

Outside of town the hideous four rendezvoused at the side of the road. Looking back toward Oracle Junction, they observed that no one was following.

"Probably won't be anyone aware of the robbery till it's time for them two employees to show up at home," observed Mack Evans.

"It'll take a while after that to put a posse together," added Otis Becker.

"You boys know what to do," the burly Evans said, spurring his mount and heading off the road at a right angle. "See you at the hideout!" Each of the others took off, abandoning the road in various directions.

The plan was to confuse and split up the inevitable posse. Each rider would proceed alone until he found a spot where his horse's hooves would not leave tracks. This could be a grassy area, where the prints would quickly disappear, or a place strewn with lava chunks. There were also many areas in this vast desert where the ground became solid, smooth rock. Once finding the appropriate spot, the rider would dismount and wrap the horse's feet in burlap sacks stuffed with old rags.

Each man had trained his horse to walk in the sacks. The soft, spongy material left only a slight surface impression. The normal crosswinds of the desert would erase them almost immediately, leaving no trace for the bewildered posse.

The riders would travel in this manner for some time, heading straight for the hideout. After putting ample distance between themselves and the place of their "disappearance," they would remove the sacks and ride hard.

The four repugnant bank robbers sat around the rickety old kitchen table, fully elated with the results of the day's work. A coal-oil lantern illuminated the room from the dusty cupboard. A bottle of rye was making the rounds.

Mack Evans had the currency piled in five stacks. In the middle was a yellowed slip of paper on which he had scribbled some figures.

Flipping the worn pencil stub aside, he said, "Okay, boys. The total take was a hunnerd and twenty-eight thousand, eight hundred and three dollars."

Neal Furman arched his bushy black eyebrows and ejected a low whistle. Otis Becker exposed his yellow teeth in a wide smile. Dick Millard rubbed his nose and eyed the loot.

"Boss gets half," continued the huge Evans, placing a grimy finger on the largest stack. "After all, if he didn't have an inside track on these money shipments, we wouldn't know where to go after it."

The other three nodded complacently.

"That leaves sixty-four thousand, four hunnerd. Divided four ways, is sixteen thousand, one hunnerd each."

Neal Furman ran his tongue around his lips.

"You each promised to pay me a thousand on every job for gettin' you on with my boss. That leaves each one of you fifteen thousand, one hunnerd," Evans continued, sliding the neatly stacked bills in three directions. Pulling the remaining stack toward himself, he added. "And nineteen thousand, one hunnerd for big Mack."

Three one-dollar bills were left in the center of the table. Evans chuckled. "And my fee for doing all this book work is three dollars. Any objections?" His eyes roved the faces of the three outlaws.

The three cohorts were satisfied. No one was about to object over a mere three dollars.

Evans upended the bottle and finished it off. The rest of the evening was spent over a card game while they intermittently discussed the next bank job.

As the game grew wearisome, Otis Becker looked at the gold watch. "Nearly eleven o'clock," he said, tiredly. "Suppose the boss ain't comin' tonight?"

"He'll be here," Evans said flatly.

No more than five minutes had passed when two of the horses nickered outside. All four outlaws were instantly on their feet.

"It's the boss," said Neal Furman.

"Probably," said Evans, drawing his gun and moving toward the door. "But we'll wait for the password."

The four men waited quietly. The soft plopping sound of hooves on smooth earth met their ears. A horse snorted.

A pungent voice penetrated the adobe walls. "*Jackrabbit!*"

Promptly Mack Evans pulled open the door. "Howdy, boss," he said, looking into the darkness.

Presently a tall, well-built man stepped into the yellow light of the lantern. His clean-shaven face, neatly trimmed hair, and clean clothing contrasted him sharply with his motley crew. His angular face and sturdily molded jaw gave him an air of authority.

"We were wonderin' if you'd make it tonight, boss," said Otis Becker, scratching his rib cage.

"Had a few things to handle first," said the square-shouldered man. "Don't dare leave any known business unattended before I slip out of town."

Mack Evans chimed in. "Got somethin' for you, boss." Reaching for the canvas bag on a chair, he walked to the table and dumped out the bundles of currency.

"How much?" asked the boss.

"Total take was a hundred twenty-eight thousand, eight hunnerd." Producing the yellowed slip of paper, he said, "Here's the figgers. You take the first half, as we agreed. We split the second half."

Mack Evans's boss plucked the paper from his thick fingers and examined it carefully. With his other hand he ruffled the packets of money, scattering them so that none lay on top of another. "The bank only had twenty-eight thousand on hand for regular business?" His eyes held Evans's gaze steadily.

The big man resented the tone of the question but suppressed it cautiously. "That's all there was, boss."

The hard lines in the taller man's face suddenly melted into a smile. "You've never cheated me, Mack. Just want to keep it that way. Last man that tricked me became buzzard meat. His bones lie half buried in the sand out at Dead Man's Gulch."

Evans forced a smile. "Boss, you know me better than that."

The formidable leader broke into a hearty laugh. All four outlaws joined in loudly.

Slapping Otis Becker's broad back, the boss said, "Hey, this is some dump! You did all right, Becker."

"I think it's gonna work out real good, boss," answered Becker.

Turning to Mack Evans, the boss said, "Any shooting today?"

"Nope. Went smooth. We left the teller and the

bookkeeper tied and gagged, along with one customer."

"Good, good," declared the boss. "Less heat on everybody if nobody gets shot." Pulling out a chair, he sat down and pulled himself up to the table. "Sit down, gentlemen," he said cheerfully. "Let's discuss what's next. We'll take the bank in Willcox and the one in Benson. Both of them have secret Fargo money. Should handle them before Sundeen arrives."

"You've heard from him?" Neal Furman asked, scratching his head.

"Yep. Wire came in today from town of Greasewood Springs, up near the Utah border. Came for Mack. I intercepted it. It was relayed through Phoenix. Said he had been delayed a few days in Green River. Should be here in a little over a week." The boss rocked his chair back on two legs. "Then we can concentrate on the Tucson job . . . *the really big money!*"

CHAPTER EIGHT

Ric Baron's knees were shaky. There was a hot pit in the middle of his stomach. The ice-blue eyes of the tall man facing him seemed to pierce his timorous soul.

"This yellow-bellied sidewinder is waiting for you to draw, punk!" Dan Colt rasped.

Every eye in the gathering crowd was fixed on Ric Baron. The kid was about to go for his guns when he heard his brother's voice coming from behind his towering adversary.

"*Hold it, Colt!*" Vic Baron shouted.

Dan did not flinch. His eyes stayed on Ric, who was now looking past him toward his older brother. Vic ran around Dan and stood between the two, facing Ric.

"Ric, this hawk is *Dan Colt!*" he said breathlessly.

The younger Baron batted his eyes. "You mean *the* Dan Colt?"

"None other. You get out of the way," Vic said, shoving his brother into the crowd. Wheeling, he faced the tall man.

"Where's Dolly?" Dan asked, baring his teeth.

"She's all right," Vic Baron said levelly.

"I asked you *where* she is, Baron."

"I'm right here, Dan!" Dolly called from the crowd to Dan's left.

Colt's ice-water eyes never strayed from the man

known as the Executioner. "Did he hurt you, Dolly?" asked Dan out of the side of his mouth.

"No, I'm all right," she answered.

Vic Baron went into his stance. His black flat-crowned hat shaded his dark eyes. "I heard you got bushwacked and dumped in a Kansas hole, Colt," said Baron.

"You heard wrong," Dan said morosely.

"Good. Your reputation has been a thorn in my gut for a long time," Baron hissed defiantly. "Now I can take care of it."

A hot wrath bolted through Dan Colt's veins. He studied Vic Baron standing before him, feet spread apart, shoulders sloped, hands at belt level, palms down. Dan had faced many a gunfighter. Always he had walked away, leaving the other man dead or dying. Some had been among the best in the business. But never had he been confronted by a challenge like the one he faced at this moment. A virulent, pitiless expression lurked in the Executioner's eyes.

The thought leaped into Dan's mind that every gunfighter had to meet an illusive, nameless figure who waited for him in some dark corner of the future. Somewhere in his path there lingered that man who was faster on the draw. Vic Baron could be that man. Quickly Dan dismissed the thought. *I'm that man in Vic Baron's path,* he told himself emphatically.

The people stood in awe. The name *Dan Colt* spread through the awestruck crowd like a prairie fire on a windy day.

"Make your play," Dan said through his teeth. A cold, calculated determination settled over him.

Ric Baron stood at the forefront of the crowd, a look of wild expectancy on his face.

Quicker than a thought Vic Baron's guns were in his hands, belching fire. One bullet whanged off a wagon wheel down the street, while the other plowed dust near the boots of the tall man whose guns had roared a split second earlier.

Dan Colt had shot him through the middle, both slugs hitting the same spot. Vic Baron jackknifed as if he had been struck in the midsection with a battering ram. His hat fell from his head as both guns slipped from limp fingers.

The seasoned Colt had put the bullets in Baron's midsection rather than his heart, calculating that he would live long enough to know what hit him. The Executioner lay on his side, legs drawn upward, breathing heavily. His face was a ghastly mask of raw terror. A steady flow of blood seeped through his clutching fingers, clotting the dust and turning it a dull brown. Dan Colt stood over him like a tall, indestructible tower. "I won't be a thorn in your gut any more, Baron," he said softly. "Something else has taken my place."

Vic Baron's eyes glassed over. He tried to speak, but the words choked in his throat. His slender legs straightened out in a final spasm of life. He rolled over, facedown. His last breath lifted a small puff of dust. Then he was still.

Ric stepped out of the crowd, a look of disbelief on his chalky-white face. Ignoring the tall man, he knelt in the dust beside his dead brother, mumbling incoherently.

Dan waited a long moment. Then he spoke harshly. "Okay, kid, you're next!"

Ric Baron tilted his face upward. Blinking his eyes, he said, "Huh?"

"I said you're next."

"I—I'm n–not gonna draw against you," he said, shaking his head.

Dan reasoned that the only way he could keep the younger Baron from ending up like his brother was to scare the gunfighter out of him here and now. "You roughed up a crippled girl, sonny. The only thing lower than a dog who would do a thing like that is the scum on a snake's belly. For that you'll draw against me. Now stand to your feet!"

Ric Baron's body trembled like a weeping willow in an earthquake. Dan reached down and sank his fingers into the frightened youth's shirt. Yanking him to his feet, he said, "Now, you *draw*!"

"No!" Ric screeched. "No! You can't make me!"

"You said I was a yellow-bellied sidewinder. What's that make you?" Dan chided him hard.

Ric pointed to his dead brother. "If I draw against you, I'll end up like that!" he said, almost in tears.

Dan reached down and yanked both guns from the kid's holsters. He broke the action and punched out the cartridges. Flipping the barrels into his hands, he stepped to the hitchrail and shattered the handles with one blow. With the second blow the hammers broke off. Dropping them in the dirt, the tall man walked back to face the horrified Ric Baron.

"That's for calling me a yellow-bellied sidewinder," he said evenly. "And this is for roughing up Dolly Wyler." His brawny fist flashed like a bolt of lightning. The kid went down like chopped timber. He lay motionless, out like a pinched wick.

Dolly Wyler limped toward the tall man and wrapped her arms around him. She looked up with relief written in her eyes. "Oh Dan, I'm so glad you're all right!"

Knuckling away a tear that had just spilled onto her cheek, he said, "Let's get you home, Dolly."

As Dan Colt and Dolly Wyler rode away together on the big black, Basil Anderson hoisted the heels of Vic Baron. Speaking to the man who had gotten ahold of the Baron's shoulders, he said, "I'm gonna run out of coffins if things don't quiet down in this bloody town." Twisting his fat neck and looking around the crowd, he said, "Where in thunder is Ches Ramsey? Town's gonna owe me for another burial before sunset."

Two men stood near the yet unconscious Ric Baron, gazing toward the pair on the black gelding. As they passed from sight, one of the men said, "Who would have believed it? All the time that Sundeen fella was the famous Dan Colt!"

"Yeah," remarked the other, "I've heard about him for years. Never dreamed I'd ever lay eyes on him. Invisible hands." The last two words were said almost to himself.

His friend turned a furrowed brow toward him. "What say?"

"I said, when it comes to drawin' them guns, he's got invisible hands!"

As the black gelding carried the tall man and the crippled girl down a long grade, the tall man said, "That clump of trees off to the right?"

"Yes," she asserted, "they left him on the far side of the trees."

Marshal Chester Ramsey was still handcuffed to the tree, turning the air a misty blue color with swear words even Dan Colt had never heard.

Dismounting and leaving Dolly on the black, he said, "Where's your key, Marshal?"

The lawman's face was dark with rage. A knot had formed on the side of his head. A rivulet of blood had streamed down his temple and dried. The dented Stetson lay beside him.

"In my vest. Watch pocket."

Dan produced the key and unlocked the cuffs.

"I'm gonna lock them two up and forget I did it," Ramsey muttered hoarsely, rubbing his chafed wrists. Standing up stiffly, he said, "I get 'em in my jail, they'll never get out."

"One of them would stink it up pretty bad," said Dan.

"Huh?" said Ramsey, squinting at him.

"Vic Baron is dead."

In his fury the marshal had forgotten the purpose for which he had been shackled to the tree. Rubbing his head, he picked up his hat. "You gun him?"

"Yep."

"What about that hatchet-faced kid?"

"Last time I saw him, he was taking a nap," Dan said casually, winking at Dolly.

Ramsey walked to the clump of grass where the outlaws had thrown his gun. After rubbing and blowing it free of dust, he holstered it and plodded off through the trees toward his horse. The sedate animal was grazing lazily in the afternoon sun. The Green River lawman led his horse to where Dan Colt stood by the black.

Dan turned and lifted his left foot. "See you later, Marshal," he said, placing the foot in the stirrup. His back was to the lawman.

As Dan threw his weight to the stirrup, Ramsey said sharply, "You're under arrest, Sundeen!"

Dropping his right foot back to earth, Dan eyed the thick-bodied marshal. The muzzle of his revolver was lined on Dan's midsection.

"What for?"

"How does *prison break* sound for starters?"

"I'm not David Sundeen," said Colt flatly.

"You don't really expect me to swaller that, do yuh?"

"It's the truth, Marshal. My name is Dan Colt. Dave Sundeen is my twin brother."

"And Davey Crockett is my grandpaw," sliced Ramsey dryly. "Dan Colt was ambushed out in Kansas. Buried by his killers in an unmarked grave."

"Not a word of truth in it, Ramsey. I—"

"Drop your gunbelt, Sundeen." Ches Ramsey's eyes were cold and hard. "Go slow. Use one hand."

When the twin Colts lay at Dan's feet, the Green River lawman said, "Now, pick 'em up careful-like and bring 'em to me."

Looping Dan's gunbelt over his pommel, Ramsey said, "Now lay down flat on your belly. Hands behind your back."

Reluctantly the tall man obeyed. Ramsey knelt down, snapping handcuffs on his wrists. Looking toward Dolly, who sat on the black, he said, "You come and ride double with me, honey. I want Sundeen on his horse alone. I'll take you home. Then I can get this outlaw in a cell."

Randy Wyler sat on a tree stump at the edge of the yard, eyes glued to the crest of the hill where the wagon trail met the road at the gate. The faith of his boyish heart was strong. There was not a doubt in his mind that Dan Colt would emerge the conqueror in the shootout with Victor Baron, in spite of Baron's first name. After all, there was a man in the Bible whose name was Daniel. He went up against a whole den full of lions . . . and walked away the victor. Daniel Colt would do the same with the Executioner.

The afternoon sun was warm on the boy's face. He thought of the blistering days of summer that would soon come. He was glad he did not live farther south, in Arizona. Down at Yuma it sometimes got up to almost a hundred and twenty degrees.

He lifted his hat and wiped sweat from his brow. As he replaced the hat, a movement caught his eyes, and he squinted against the sharp rays of the sun. There were two horses, three riders. Within a minute Randy focused on the black gelding and the tall form on its back. Dolly's long blond hair was visible, flowing in the breeze.

Bounding across the yard, he ran toward the house. "Mama! Mama! It's Dolly and Dan! They're comin'!"

Clara Wyler dashed through the door and onto the porch, the elderly man at her heels. Both hastened toward the excited boy, looking past him to the riders descending the grassy slope. Within half a minute Molly Jo had joined them.

Tears welled up in Clara's eyes. "Oh, thank the dear Lord!" she exclaimed. "Our prayers are answered!"

"Looks like Marshal Ramsey, Clara," said John Wyler.

Molly Jo was weeping and waving both hands. Randy followed suit.

As the horses drew nearer, Clara's gaze caught the sight of Dan's hands cuffed behind his back and the black gelding being led by the marshal. "Gramps," she said gravely, "he's got Dan shackled."

The old man squinted. "By cracky, Clara, you're right."

Slowly Ches Ramsey dismounted and helped Dolly from the horse. As Clara embraced the crippled girl, she eyed Dan, then flashed her gaze to the marshal.

"Marshal Ramsey, why is Dan handcuffed?" she demanded.

"'Cuz he ain't Dan Colt, ma'am. He's Dave Sundeen. Wanted down in Arizona."

Molly Jo's eyes bolted the lawman with fire. Anger welled up in her voice. "He is *not* Dave Sundeen! He *is* Dan Colt! You're making a big mistake, Marshal. You—"

"I've been telling him that," interrupted Dolly, "but he won't listen." Breaking into tears, the girl sobbed, "Oh Mama, tell him! Don't let him put Dan in jail!"

For several moments the five Wylers argued eloquently on Dan Colt's behalf but to no avail.

Climbing into his saddle, Ches Ramsey said calmly, "I'm sorry folks. I'm not the judge nor the jury. My job is to take him in. There's a U.S. marshal on his way now to take him back to Yuma."

Dan's face tightened. "You don't mean Logan Tanner?"

"Yep. The same."

The Wyler family stood motionlessly in stunned silence as they watched the two men ride away.

The red sun threw a long shadow on the east side of the fresh mound as Ric Baron stood slump-shouldered over his brother's grave. The clatter of Basil Anderson's empty wagon faded slowly away. The wind whipped across Boot Hill, playing a mournful dirge. Hot tears scalded young Baron's cheeks.

His lower lip quivered as he cast a lamentable look at the grave and said, "I'll kill him for you, Vic. I promise. You may not like the way I do it, but he'll be dead. He'll pay for what he did."

The wind carried a nicker from the road. Ric Baron rubbed the moisture from his eyes and turned to look as his own horse answered the nicker.

The man who had outdrawn and gunned down his brother was riding a black gelding, which was being led by the town marshal. Dan Colt's hands were fettered behind him. The twin .45's that had spit death to Vic Baron were swinging loosely on the marshal's pommel.

Briefly the two riders eyed Ric Baron in passing, but neither lingered in his gaze.

"This is gonna be easier than I thought," said Ric to the mound. "He ain't even got his guns, Vic, he—"

Ric's hands fell to his empty holsters. He swore heavily, remembering that Colt had destroyed his guns. He swore again when he thought of Basil Anderson's refusal to give him Vic's guns, saying that he could have them after Anderson got paid for the burial. He swore a third time when he shot a glance to his empty saddle boot. He had left the rifle in the hotel room.

Looking again toward the grave of his fallen brother, he said vehemently, "I'll get him, Vic. Don't you worry none. He put my brother in Boot Hill. I'll do the same to him. I'll dance on his grave. That's what I'll do. I'll dance on his grave!"

CHAPTER NINE

Sunset stained the valley a brilliant fiery crimson and then gradually blended the long shadows into an exquisite purple. For a long moment the purple thickness hovered defiantly, then reluctantly surrendered to the soft shades of night.

Stretched out on the cot in his cell, Dan Colt listened to the early sounds of gaiety filtering through the night air. Soon the saloons would be in full swing.

He should have been in Arizona by now, breathing down Dave Sundeen's outlaw neck. Was this another quirk of fate? How long was this going to continue? A few days ago he was practically tasting Dave's dust. Now the outlaw twin was probably a hundred miles away, maybe more. What inscrutable force of destiny rode his path to hinder him? Would this vexatious millstone never be released from his neck?

Dan Colt rued the day he had ridden into Holbrook, Arizona. It was there that he had been mistaken for Dave Sundeen and arrested by Logan Tanner. Five months he had spent in that fragment of hell on earth called Yuma Territorial Prison. Now, seven months later, he was no closer to clearing himself than the night he escaped from Yuma.

Logan Tanner, like a slobbering bloodhound, would be in Green River shortly. *Somehow,* Dan told himself, *I've got to break out of here before Tanner arrives.*

After wolfing down a supper provided by the town,

Dan lay in the dark with his thoughts. By eleven o'clock Ches Ramsey had snuffed the lights in the office and drifted off to sleep. Suddenly Dan heard a shuffling noise outside the cell window.

Quietly he moved to the wall beneath the window and listened. Something was brushing against the building. Presently a whisper penetrated the shuttered covering.

"Dan! Dan!"

Cautiously swinging open the window covering, Dan whispered in response. "Who is it?"

A heavy wire mesh covered the bars. In the dim light that emanated from a half moon, a face appeared. The base of the window was seven feet from the floor. The opening was one foot square. Dan could not make out the features.

"It's Molly Jo," came the whispered answer. "I've brought you a gun."

"I can't involve you in this," Dan breathed heavily. "You could go to prison for helping me."

"I can't let them take you back to Yuma."

Standing tiptoe, Dan said, "I'll find another way. You scat quick, before the marshal wakes up!"

"I have some wire-cutters," whispered Molly Jo, ignoring Dan's command. "I'll cut a hole and pass the gun through."

"What are you standing on?"

"My horse. Is the marshal still sleeping?"

"Just a second." Dan glided quietly across the cell to the door. He could hear the steady snoring of Ches Ramsey filtering through the wooden door that separated the cell area from the office. Returning to the window, he whispered, "Yeah. Like a baby."

"I'll be as quiet as I can," she said. Her words were immediately followed by the sudden snap of heavy wire. The sound was repeated in broken intervals, purposely timed to allow Dan to listen for movement in the front office.

In less than five minutes, which seemed like an hour, the butt of a Navy Colt .45 protruded through the opening. Dan felt the cold grips in his sweaty palm.

"The rest is up to you," Molly Jo whispered.

"Does your mother know you're doing this?"

"No. I climbed out my bedroom window."

"Then you get on back right away, do you hear?"

"Yes."

"Molly Jo."

"Yes?"

"Find something to rub out the hoofprints. Every shoe leaves an identifying mark."

"Okay."

"Rub them out all the way to the street."

"I will."

"Molly Jo."

"Yes?"

"Thanks!"

"Dan?"

"Yes?"

"*I love you!*"

With that statement fresh in Dan Colt's ears, Molly Jo Wyler was gone.

Fingering the gun in the dark, Dan satisfied himself that it was fully loaded. The last thing he wanted to do was use it on Ches Ramsey, but Ramsey must not know it. When Green River's lone lawman looked down the barrel of the Navy Colt, he must see a fully loaded chamber.

From outside it sounded like Molly Jo had found a broom. She would obliterate the hoofprints and be on her way home. When the sweeping sound ceased, Dan waited about five minutes.

On a small table in his cell sat a large water-pitcher. Holding the pistol in one hand, he lifted the pitcher with the other and slammed it savagely to the floor. It shattered with a loud crash. Momentarily Dan heard Ramsey mumbling something indistinguishable, then a yellow shaft of light appeared under the door.

As Ramsey entered the passageway outside the cell door, Dan flattened himself against the wall adjacent to the bars. Sleepily the marshal held the lantern level with his face and approached the bars. A revolver hung loosely in his other hand.

"What's going on in here?" Ramsey demanded, trying to clear his vision.

Suddenly he was looking at a gun muzzle as the hammer made a double clicking sound. His vision cleared and his jaw slackened.

"Drop the gun, Marshal," Dan said gruffly. "Set the lantern down."

"How—?"

"Never mind. Just lift the keys off the hook over there by the door and open the cell."

Ramsey complied wearily. When the door opened, grating on its hinges, Dan stepped out and kicked Ramsey's gun through the doorway and into the outer office. He handcuffed the lawman to the metal cot and gagged him carefully. "I don't like doing this to you, Marshal, but you left me no choice. The only way I can prove I am not Dave Sundeen is to produce Dave Sundeen. I can't do that while rotting at Yuma."

Dan locked the cell door and hung the keys on the hook. Carrying the lantern into the office, he located his twin Colts and strapped them on, thonging the holsters to his thighs. Jamming the Navy Colt under his belt, he picked up a pencil and hastily wrote a note. Folding it neatly, he slipped the note into his shirt pocket. Taking another piece of paper, he wrote in large letters:

> MARSHAL OUT.
> BACK LATER.

Attaching the sign to the door window so as to be read from the outside, he donned his hat and blew out the lamp.

The night air was stimulating. It felt good to his lungs. Green River was fast asleep.

Making a beeline for the back of the jail, Dan hastened along the back of the buildings lining that side of the street. When he reached the corner he eyed the livery stable in the pale moonlight. It stood diagonally across the street. In five seconds he was swinging his leg over the corral fence. Several horses were confined in the small area. Spotting the black gelding was easy in the dim light. The white blaze and four white stockings seemed to glow against the night.

Entering the shed, Dan struck a match. Spying his bridle and saddle, he blew out the light and carried them outside. One of the horses whinnied and another answered. Dan shot a glance toward the hostler's shack as he spread the blanket on the gelding's broad back. In a moment the cinch was tight and the bridle in place.

Leading the magnificent animal, he unlatched the gate. The hinges whined noisily. With haste the tall man swung the gate shut and dropped the latch. Once more he glanced at the shack. All was still.

In one smooth move Dan Colt was in the saddle and heading north at a full gallop. The big horse settled into an even glide as the wind whistled in Dan's ears. The pale light of the moon cast an eerie glow over Boot Hill as horse and rider passed by. Dan thought of Vic Baron lying cold beneath the sod.

He reined the gelding to a trot as he approached the gate of the Wyler ranch. Passing through the gate, he descended the long slope and cut the horse to a walk. About fifty yards from the house he dismounted and approached the back porch on foot. He was glad the Wylers did not have a dog.

Carefully he lifted a wooden chair and placed it directly in front of the door. Slipping the note from his pocket, he opened it and angled it toward the moon. He read it through, making sure it was worded correctly:

> *Have to move fast. U.S. marshal on my trail. Heading for Tombstone. After I find Dave and clear myself, I'll be back. Hope you'll be able to sell house and get Dolly to Denver. I'll find you. Thanks to M.J. for the help.*
>
> *Dan*

Placing the note on the seat of the chair, he laid the Navy Colt on top of it.

Briskly he made his way around the house toward the black gelding. As he approached the horse, it nickered. Standing next to it was Molly Jo, her long blond hair shimmering softly in the moonlight. She was wearing a dark robe that brushed the tops of her slippered feet. Dan could hear the slight chatter of her teeth.

"You silly kid," said Dan, shaking his head, "you're gonna catch pneumonia. How did you know I was coming here?"

"I didn't. I just got back into my room and was getting ready for bed in the dark when I saw you ride in."

"I left the gun and a note on the porch," he said softly. "Thanks again for helping me. Now you get back in the house."

Moving swiftly Molly Jo flung herself against Dan's

muscular frame and clung to him fiercely. "Oh Dan," she breathed, "promise you'll come back to me!"

Gripping her shoulders and forcing her slowly from him, he said, "Molly Jo, when I do come back, it will be as a friend of the family."

The tears in her eyes reflected the milky light in the sky. "But Dan, I'm in love with you. Don't you feel—"

"You're in love with love, little lady. Less than a week ago it was Dave. You're young, Molly Jo. You've got a lot of time to be in and out of love yet."

She opened her mouth to speak, but Dan continued.

"When you really do find that right fella . . . he will be closer to your own age."

"But . . ."

"You get in the house now. Tell your mother I'm sorry I couldn't stay long enough to finish the paint job."

"But . . ."

"Tell Dolly I'm coming back someday. I want to see her walk after the operation."

"But Dan, when will you come back?"

"After I turn Dave over to the authorities."

"That could be—"

"A long time? Yes, it could be. If you're not here, I'll look you up in Denver. Now you *git*."

Tilting her face upward, he kissed her forehead. "So long, kid."

Quickly he mounted the gelding. Molly Jo stood there, shivering. Dan gave her a stern look. "Go on. I'll wait till you're safe in the house."

Slowly the girl turned and walked toward the house without looking back. When she disappeared through the window, Dan touched his spurs to the gelding's sides and headed up the moonlit slope.

* * *

Ric Baron left the hotel lobby, rifle in hand, and stepped into the bright morning sunlight. Earlier he had gone to the livery and saddled his horse. Basil Anderson was not in his place of business yet, so Baron had returned to the dining room for breakfast.

It was now nearly eight thirty. *Anderson had better be there by now,* Baron thought. Sliding the rifle into the saddle boot, he mounted and rode to the furniture shop that doubled as an undertaking parlor. This time the fat man was in.

Ric Baron passed through the front door and made his way to the back room. Anderson was bending over his workbench.

"I want my brother's guns—now," Baron said stiffly.

Anderson gave him a sour look. "Town hasn't paid me yet. I'll see the marshal in a little while and—"

"I said *now!*" Baron's face was florid and hard.

"Now look here, kid, you'll get the guns when I get paid. Come back in a couple hours." With that, the flabby undertaker turned back to his task.

A heavy claw-hammer, mingled with an assortment of tools on a table behind Anderson, caught Ric Baron's eye. Moving swiftly he gripped the handle with both hands. The fat man turned his head just as Baron brought the hammer down full force.

Basil Anderson dodged just enough to make the hammer glance off his temple. Slightly stunned, he grabbed a large chisel and swung it in a wide arc toward the kid's midsection. The lithe youth moved away quickly. The sharp instrument sliced nothing but air.

Again Baron struck at Anderson's head. This time the hammer hit squarely with a hollow thumping sound. The heavy man staggered, but before Ric could bring the hammer to bear again, Anderson slammed his massive body into the kid's lean frame.

Breath whooshed from Baron's lungs and he lost his footing. As he rolled onto the floor, the big man lunged for him, swinging the sharp chisel as he would a butcher knife. Anderson was still off balance from the second blow. He stumbled and missed Baron completely.

From a kneeling position the slender youth thudded Anderson's head again. The bulky undertaker hit the floor and rolled. Baron swung and hit him again. This time the hammer struck him at the fleshy base of his skull. The chisel clattered to the floor.

Anderson, breathing heavily, reached for the chisel. The hammer caught him on the side of the head, puncturing the skin. Blood spurted, flowing freely.

Baron quickly picked up the chisel and gained his feet, sucking in air. Anderson was up on one knee, shaking his bloodsmeared head. Like a mortally wounded beast, he charged blindly. The kid braced himself for the impact, holding the chisel stiffly. A half-step before the fat man reached him, Baron thrust the chisel into his belly. Anderson ejected a heavy grunt, eyes bulging, mouth gaping. From the folds of fat around the chisel, Ric Baron felt a warm, sticky fluid engulf his hand.

Anderson's bulky frame swayed slightly. Baron let the bloody handle slip from his fingers. The heavy man let out a death cry and crumpled to the floor.

Ric Baron stood looking at his blooddrenched hand when he suddenly became aware of the door closing out front. The sound of footsteps coming toward the back room blended with a man's masculine voice. "Basil! You back there?"

Wildly the young Baron retrieved the hammer and flattened himself against the wall next to the doorway. Holding the hammer with both hands, he lifted it above his head, ready to strike.

The unidentified intruder emerged through the door. "I say, Basil, are you—" His eyes fell to the bloodsoaked body of Basil Anderson.

The hammer dropped savagely, sending the man to the floor in a lifeless heap.

Quickly Baron moved to the wash basin. Pouring water from the nearby pitcher, he frantically washed the blood from his hand. Some had splattered on his vest and shirt, but both were dark and it would go unnoticed. He dried with a towel that hung on an old nail nearby.

In less than a minute he found his brother's guns in a wooden cabinet. Stepping over the lifeless heap in the inner doorway, he moved toward the outside door. A tattered sign hung in the door window on a piece of string. The back side said CLOSED. He flipped the back side forward, holstered Vic's guns on his hips, and opened the door.

Carefully he looked both ways. A buckboard was coming up the street. He closed the door and moved back into the shadows. Presently the buckboard idled by and he opened the door again. There were people moving about, but no one near enough to notice him. A crowd seemed to be gathering down the street.

Casually Ric Baron walked to his horse, looped the empty holsters over the pommel, and mounted up. He rode slowly toward the marshal's office. His mind was bent on one thing: *He must kill Dan Colt.*

He would saunter into the office and get the lawman into a conversation. At the proper moment he would get the drop on him. At gunpoint he would make him turn around. A gunbarrel across his head would leave Baron free to move to the cell area and blow Colt to kingdom come.

A tight smile crossed his lips. It would be like shooting a great big fish in a little tiny barrel.

The accumulating crowd proved to be clustering at

the marshal's office. Ric Baron dismounted at the fringe of the crowd. Looping the reins around the hitchrail he eyed two men who were speaking excitedly in front of the office door. One was Marshal Ches Ramsey. The other was a broad-shouldered, thick-bodied man in his late forties. He was handsome in a rugged sort of way and wore a heavy moustache that was salted with gray, as were his temples and sideburns. On his leather vest was a silver shield bearing the deep inscription UNITED STATES MARSHAL.

Baron spoke to a middle-aged man who stood nearby. "What's all the fuss?"

"Prisoner escaped," said the man. "That Dan Colt fella. The one who gunned your brother. He locked the marshal in his own jail and took off. Must've been late last night."

"Anybody know which way he went?" Baron asked, a defeated feeling washing over him.

"Nope."

"Who's the federal dude?"

"Name's Tanner. He's the one found Ramsey. Seems Tanner's been on Colt's trail. Prison break."

A petulant frustration ran through Ric Baron's system like a straight shot of raw whiskey. Killing Dan Colt in the jail would have been so simple. Now he would have to track him down and wait for the proper opportunity.

Deep in thought, the young Baron slid into the saddle and headed north out of town.

The sun was approaching the midway point in the morning sky when Ric Baron rode through the gate on the Wyler ranch.

The old man and the boy were engrossed in painting the barn. No one else was in sight. Baron rode to the barn.

John Wyler was standing on the fourth rung of a ladder, applying paint just above the barn doors.

Randy was painting the handles on the door. Neither had noticed Baron's approach.

"Hey, old man!" Ric bellowed. "Where's Colt?"

Wyler, startled at the unexpected utterance, dropped his paint brush. "You don't have to holler," the old man snapped. "I ain't deef!"

Randy picked up the fallen paint brush from the dirt and wiped it on an old rag. The silver-haired Wyler stepped to the ground.

"I asked you a question, grandpaw," said Baron rudely. "I'm waiting for an answer."

John Wyler slung a hard look at the ostentatious youth. "You've seen the Green River just east of here?"

"Yeah."

"Go jump in it." The elderly man's jaw was set in an unyielding line.

Fire ignited in Baron's eyes. Leaping off the horse, he unholstered one of his revolvers and drew a bead between Wyler's eyes. "Guess you're tired of livin', huh, grandpaw?" he asked coldly, thumbing back the hammer.

"Nope. But I ain't scared o' dyin' neither," retorted Wyler without blinking an eye. "You're really rough, tough stuff, ain'tcha?"

"What do you mean?" said Baron, narrowing his eyes.

"You can face an unarmed old man four times your age, but you sure turned chicken-liver yellow when Dan Colt braced you."

Ric Baron's face flushed.

"Yeah," chimed in Randy. "Dolly told us how you showed everybody in town the big yellow stripe down your back!"

"You shut up, kid," Baron rasped with bared teeth. "Now where's Colt?" His glare bolted hard on John Wyler.

"How should I know? He doesn't report to me. Last

time I saw him, he was ridin' handcuffed, goin' to jail in Green River."

"He broke jail and you know it," Baron said, stepping closer. "Now, old man, I'm gonna ask you one more time. *Where's Dan Colt?*"

"What do you want him for? To shoot him in the back? You sure ain't gonna face him."

Angrily Baron swung the muzzle to the right and fired. The bullet missed the old man's left ear, tearing into the barn. "Next one will be between the eyes," the youth said menacingly as he thumbed back the hammer again.

Wyler did not flinch.

Quickly Baron lifted the muzzle and fired again, the shot going just above Wyler's silver hair.

Randy, in a state of panic, blurted out, "He went to Tombstone!" Running between Baron and his grandfather, he faced the gunman. "Now get out of here and let us alone!"

"You better not be lying. If I find out you lied, I'll come back and kill you." Ric Baron's dark eyes held the boy hard.

"I ain't lying. He left a note saying he was headed for Tombstone."

"Fetch me the note, kid. I want to see it."

"*Get on your horse and ride!*" Clara Wyler's voice sliced the air.

Baron wheeled to face the muzzle of Clara's Winchester. He still held the gun in his hand, but it was pointed toward the ground. He knew full well she could fire before he could lift it and shoot her. The look in her eyes left no doubt that she would do it.

A wicked grin curled Baron's thin lips. "Okay, ma'am," he said with a sneer. "I got what I wanted." He walked toward the horse, holstering the revolver. Clara's rifle followed him.

"Dan Colt will lead-gut you, mister," said Randy icily. "He'll plant you in Boot Hill with your brother."

"We'll see about that," retorted Ric Baron, reining his mount in a tight circle. "We'll see about that," he repeated and galloped away.

CHAPTER TEN

Black thunderheads were gathering rapidly, hiding the jagged peaks of the San Juan Mountains. Dan Colt knew as he ascended the foothills that the rain would begin any minute. If a posse from Green River was on his trail, the rain would exterminate his tracks.

He questioned that a posse would come. Logan Tanner no doubt would insist on carrying out the pursuit alone. Tracking him through these mountains would be extremely difficult in good weather. The rain would make it next to impossible.

The wind was picking up. As the sky became like ebony, it was evident that darkness would come early.

Lightning splintered out of the murky clouds, followed by a piercing clap of thunder. The big black gelding flicked its ears nervously. The towering pine and spruce trees swayed heavily in the wind. Dan reined the horse to a stop and removed his slicker from the saddle pack. He sighed heavily as he was reminded that the pack contained no food. There had been no time to stock up. The canteen was about half-full of three-day-old water.

Horse and rider continued climbing. Another jagged shaft of lightning cut the sky just ahead of them. Quickly a sharp boom of thunder retaliated.

A cold, misty rain descended, blanketing the earth in a shroud of water. Again a blue-white dagger lanced the air, this time striking dangerously low. Horse and rider continued to climb.

Dan Colt would never have found the man if he had not spotted the bay gelding, saddled, reins trailing, standing in a hollow some fifty yards off the trail. The horse snorted repeatedly and stamped the ground nervously.

Dan turned the black gelding toward the bay and rode into the hollow. He noticed the hindquarters of the bay were cut and bleeding slightly. At the bottom of the hollow lay a man, pressed to the earth under the weight of a fallen tree. He was conscious but stunned. Dismounting, he kneeled beside the man, who looked at him with glassy eyes.

"Can you move at all?" Dan asked with concern.

Blinking against the blur, the man said with a thick tongue, "Lightning . . . hit tree. . . ."

"Can you move?" Dan repeated.

"Don't . . . think so. . . ."

It was evident to Dan Colt that the giant pine was too heavy for him to remove by himself. Springing to his feet, he ran to the bay and removed a lariat from its saddle. Wrapping a length of the rope around the trunk of the tree and tying it securely, he backed both horses close. He attached one end of the rope to one saddle and the remaining end to the other. Grasping a bridle in each hand, he urged the horses forward. Slowly the pine lifted, rolled slightly, and came to rest.

Dan returned to the fallen rider, who now was free. Carefully he hoisted him upward and carried him out of the open draw to the shelter of the dense trees. The rain was coming down hard now. The man grimaced with pain as Dan lowered him onto the carpet of pine needles that lay beneath the trees. Lightning flashed again. Thunder roared.

"Where's your pain, friend?" Dan asked.

"Left . . . shoulder. . . . Tree came down fast. Was going to make camp in hollow. How's . . . how's my horse?"

"He's all right," answered Dan. "Scratched up a little on the rump. Nothing serious."

The man tried to adjust himself to ease the pain.

"I'll unsaddle the horses and see if I can't make you more comfortable," Dan said, walking away.

Darkness came early, as Dan had expected. By the time it was too dark to see, the injured man had his saddle for a pillow and was reasonably comfortable. There was no dry wood to build a fire, but the two men shared fresh water from the canteen on the bay's saddle and some beef jerky, along with hardtack.

About midnight the rain stopped. Dan heard a few moans through the night, but the man seemed to rest reasonably well. In the wee hours he fell asleep.

When Dan opened his eyes, the yellow light from the east threw long, slanting shadows among the tall trees. The horses were munching on grass. Periodically a gust of wind would twist the treetops, showering the earth below with water.

The injured man was looking at Dan and smiling.

"Hey, pardner," said the tall Colt, sitting up, "how is it this morning?"

"Shoulder's pretty stiff and sore," answered the man, "but the pain has eased up. I can move it some."

Dan stood up and stretched.

"My name's Joe Welby. I sure want to thank you, Mister—"

"Colt. Dan Colt," said the tall man.

Joe Welby squinted against the morning sun, cocking his head to the side. He studied the suntanned face of his rescuer. "You don't mean the famous fastgun?"

Dan rubbed the bristly stubble on his jaw. "I guess some folks might put it that way," he said vapidly.

"Weren't you supposed to have been cut down in some kind of ambush out Kansas way?"

"Some kind of rumor. I got married. Moved to Wyoming. Hung up my guns. Took up ranching."

Welby's eyes fastened on the twin Colts thonged to Dan's thighs. "Looks like you unhung 'em."

"Long story," said Dan, donning his hat. He was not interested in telling this stranger the account of Mary's murder and the details of the events that followed it. "Think you can ride?"

"Don't know," answered Welby as he rolled sideways, rose to his knees, and stood up. His left arm hung limply at his side. He stood swaying for a moment. Dan saw his face go white. His knees buckled and Dan caught him.

Joe Welby had passed out. Laying him carefully on the ground, Dan examined the shoulder. One look confirmed his suspicions: The shoulder had taken a powerful wallop. It was definitely dislocated, maybe broken. The man was going to need a doctor's care.

Another quirk of fate's pitiless hand, Dan thought to himself. Something else had arisen to delay his pursuit of Dave Sundeen. He had no choice. The only right thing to do was to take Joe Welby to the doctor in Green River.

After a cold breakfast Dan fashioned a travois, Indian-style, with two pine branches and the blankets from Welby's bedroll. Since the injured man would have to travel slowly anyway, Dan planned to stay off the trail. He would avoid the road once they were down to level ground. Chances were strong that he would run into Logan Tanner.

Thinking of the miles he could be covering in the other direction, Dan fostered evil thoughts about that foul bolt of lightning. His thinking would have been reversed if he had known that just before sunrise Ric Baron had passed by the hollow where he slept. In the firing chamber of Baron's Winchester was a forty-four caliber bullet intended for Dan Colt's back.

Dave Sundeen was still thinking of Molly Jo Wyler as Tombstone came into view on the southern horizon. There it was, houses scattered on the rugged hillside, business district on the eastern lower level. He wondered why this forlorn spot in southern Arizona Territory had become the toughest town in the West. *The place was well named,* he thought.

Halting the huge buckskin gelding, he took a long drink from his canteen. Spring had come to the desert, with the promise of an early summer. The right side of his face was hot from the late afternoon sun.

Molly Jo's pretty face filtered back into his thoughts. He had done a lot of wicked things in his time, but destroying a young girl's life was something he would not do. Why would a kid barely out of her teens be interested in a man in his thirties? He wondered how she would have felt if she knew he was an outlaw. The only thing he could do was ride out of her life.

The sun was lowering toward the western hills as Dave rode into Tombstone. He eyed Boot Hill warily as the buckskin carried him by. Every man who lived by the gun knew that death never ceased to look over his shoulder. Lawmen were buried with honor in the graceful town cemetery. Outlaws and gunslingers of Dave Sundeen's cut were roughly planted at Boot Hill in disgrace, like a rancher would bury a mangy coyote. The only difference was that at Boot Hill there was a cheap pine box and a crude grave marker. At least a coyote didn't rate those two items.

Sundeen lashed himself with a whipcord thought. *You chose this life, mister. Nobody forced it on you. You could have been a respectable citizen. When they plant your carcass in some Boot Hill, it'll be nobody's fault but your own.*

The tall, handsome outlaw had told himself many times that it was too late to change. He was a wanted man. There was a price on his head. There was nothing to do now but follow the chosen course to its bitter end. He would go on dodging lawmen and bounty hunters, would continue shooting it out with self-confident would-be gunslingers. He would keep on robbing for money until that inevitable bullet slammed the life from his body. They would carry his corpse to Boot Hill, and there would be no one to even shed a tear.

As he rode up Allen Street, Sundeen's thoughts were interrupted by the sound of loud voices in front of the Capitol Saloon. A brief glance told him that four hard-looking gunmen were in a serious dispute with one man who faced them alone. Dave approached the scene slowly and slipped quietly from the saddle. Melting into the crowd that lined the boardwalk, he positioned himself for a look at the lone man. A sheriff's star clung to his vest. He stood in the middle of the street, hand poised over the big iron slung low on his hip. The argument was reaching the boiling point.

Sundeen spoke to a tall, square-shouldered man who was dressed expensively. "What's the ruckus about?"

"The four hardcases just busted the saloon up and were about to leave. Sheriff John Springer, there, told them they would have to pay the damages. They say they won't. Looks like a shootout."

Sundeen's tanned brow furrowed. "Ain't somebody gonna help him? It's four against one."

"Both deputies are out of town," the distinguished-looking man said coldly.

The four rowdies lined up abreast, facing the tall,

determined lawman. "We ain't payin', Sheriff," said one of the unkempt gunmen. "You can either walk away and let us ride out or die in a hail of lead. Choice is yours."

The other three nodded, hands hovering over gun-butts.

"You may get me, mister," snapped John Springer, "but I'll take two of you with me. Which two will it be?" Springer's insides were churning.

"It'll be all four," said Dave Sundeen evenly, stepping up beside the sheriff. "I'll take the other two."

Without shifting his line of sight, Springer spoke from the side of his mouth. "I don't know you, friend, but you sure are welcome."

Dave Sundeen held no particular fondness for lawmen, but his natural sense of fairness impelled him to help even up the odds.

"This ain't your affair, big man!" one shouted at Dave. "You ain't wearin' no star!"

"I just made it my affair," replied Dave in an even tone. "Now you jackals fork over whatever the damages total, or Boot Hill will welcome you in short order." The square line of his jaw hardened as the familiar surge of violence warmed his blood.

One of the four lowered his voice so that only his cohorts could hear. "The gunhawk is Dan Colt. I know his face. He's fast. Too fast. I'm for gettin' out of this now."

"You plant your feet, Hawkins," growled the biggest of the four.

"But Hank, Colt is like greased lightning. He—"

"If you turn and run, I'll cut your spine in two!" the big man snapped hoarsely. "There's four of us. Two of them. We can take 'em."

"Drop your gunbelts, boys," said John Springer. "You can have your conversation after you pay Mr. Teal for the damages."

"We ain't payin'," said big Hank, his words a deep grumble.

The crowd, which lined both sides of the street, stood with bated breath.

"You want the money, lawman, you'll have to take it off our dead bodies," sliced Hank. Chuckling, he added, "That is, if you're alive to do it." His huge, beefy hand dangled over the gun on his hip.

From the side of his mouth Sundeen said in a half-whisper, "I'll start from the right and work toward the middle, you—"

The big man's hand was moving fast. A woman in the crowd screamed as guns roared.

Dave Sundeen was dropping his third man when he heard the sheriff grunt with pain. The man to his far left had taken Springer's bullet, staggered heavily, and fired at the lawman before he went down. Sundeen knew the sheriff was hit, but Springer's man was rolling over and bringing his gun to bear. Sundeen's left-hand Colt roared again. A dark hole suddenly appeared in the middle of the man's forehead. His face slammed into the dust and he lay motionless, as did his cohorts.

Instantly the crowd came alive. A number of men bounded from the boardwalks, moving through the acrid blue smoke that hung in the air.

Dave Sundeen knelt beside the fallen sheriff. Springer's left shoulder was oozing blood, soaking his shirt. He looked Sundeen in the eye. "That's some shootin', mister," he said, grimacing. "They'd have killed me for sure if you hadn't stepped in."

"Here comes the doctor!" said a voice from the encircling throng.

A hatless middle-aged man carrying a black bag elbowed his way through the crowd. "Stand back, folks," he said with a note of authority. "Give him some air!" The physician dropped to his knees, flashed Sundeen a churlish look, and rasped, "I said give him some air."

"This man . . . saved my life, doc," said Springer, his lips dry. "Those buzzards would have killed me . . . if . . . if he hadn't helped."

The doctor's countenance took on a softer expression as his eyes met Dave's briefly. Turning to examine the wound, he said, "Mighty neighborly of you to step in, stranger."

"Couldn't stand by and watch wholesale slaughter," Dave said almost casually.

"Bullet's lodged next to the armpit, John," said the doctor. "We'll get you over to the office."

John Springer's well-built frame was hoisted upward by strong hands. He managed a smile as he said to Dave Sundeen, "I don't even know your name, stranger."

"Not important," answered Sundeen. "Main thing is that you're still alive."

As the wounded sheriff was carried away, several men converged on the tall blond gunslinger, patting his broad back and pouring out congratulations. Sundeen carefully reloaded both .45's and, nodding courteously to the crowd, stepped toward the saloon.

A well-dressed, wide-shouldered man of fifty moved forward to meet him as he reached the boardwalk. Extending his hand and smiling, he said, "I'm Roy Teal, stranger. I own the Capitol, here. I'm in your debt. Those hardcases had just about enough money among them to cover the damages."

Dave met his grasp, a faint smile on his lips.

"Can I offer you a drink?" asked Teal as their hands parted.

"Guess you can," replied the tall man.

Teal followed Sundeen through the batwings. As Dave's eyes adjusted to the dim light of the saloon, he saw the barkeep brushing shattered glass into a cardboard box from the shelf behind the bar. Two other men were collecting fragments of broken furniture from the floor.

The mirror behind the bar had been reduced to a few jagged shards, which still clung tenaciously to the bullet-riddled wall. The few liquor bottles that had escaped the bombardment were standing temporarily on the bar.

"Got any glasses left, Bert?" asked Roy Teal.

"Sure, boss," replied the bartender. Reaching under the bar, he produced a pair of shot glasses.

"Bert, I want you to shake hands with the fastest gunhawk I ever saw slap leather," said Teal.

"Yeah, I saw him," said the squat, balding barkeep, gripping Sundeen's hand. "Name's Bert Riley." Riley waited for the tall man to volunteer his name. There was a dead silence. Shaking his head, Riley broke the silence. "You had those three yokels dead before they felt the grips on their guns. I admire that kind of shootin'."

"What'll it be, stranger?" asked Teal, his hand hovering over the bottles.

"Whiskey."

"Whiskey it is." Teal poured both glasses half-full.

Sundeen downed his in one toss and thumped the glass on the bar. "Either of you know a Mack Evans?"

Riley's balding scalp tightened. His eyes shifted to Teal's face. The owner of the Capitol Saloon showed no change of expression.

"Name's not familiar to me," said Teal calmly.

Sundeen's ice-blue eyes were fastened on the bartender.

"There's a big fella with a heavy mop o' gray hair comes in every now and then," Riley said advisedly. "I think that's his name."

"Any idea where I can find him?" Dave's gaze held Riley.

"Can you come back around ten o'clock tonight?" asked the balding man. "Let me do a little checkin' for you."

"Fine. I appreciate it," said Sundeen. "Thanks for the drink, Mr. Teal."

"My pleasure," said Teal. "Thank *you* for helping our sheriff."

As Dave reached the batwings, Bert Riley said, "Uh . . . where will you be staying, stranger?"

"One of the hotels," said Sundeen, pausing momentarily. "Can you suggest one?"

"The Arizona is about the best in town," replied Riley. "It's at Fifth and Allen."

"Much obliged," said the tall man warmly. The batwings squeaked and made their familiar flapping sound.

CHAPTER ELEVEN

Dave Sundeen left the buckskin at the O.K. Corral and walked to the Arizona Hotel. Evening was settling upon Tombstone as he stepped through the door of the lobby.

The desk clerk, a small, mousey-looking man with thick spectacles, greeted him with a smile. "Good evening, sir. Would you like a room?"

"Yeah," answered the tall man, "and some hot water for a bath." He adjusted the saddlebags that were draped over his shoulder.

"Yes, sir! You just sign the register, there, and we'll fix you right up."

Sundeen accepted the freshly dipped pen from the hand of the clerk. While the pen made a scratching sound, the little man said, "That sure was some fancy shooting you did today, Mr.—" His eyes dropped to the register. "Mr. . . . *Smith*." A skeptical expression formed on the clerk's pinched face. "*John Smith?*"

"You don't like my name?" asked Sundeen, his pale blue eyes bolting the little man stiffly.

"Oh . . . uh . . . no—I mean *yes!*" he answered nervously. "It's just that I've never met anybody whose real name was John Smith."

Evading Sundeen's impatient stare, the little man turned and slipped a key from its place in the maze of wall slots. Without looking Dave in the eye, he laid the key on the counter. "Room number three, Mr. Smith. The porter will bring a tub to your room right away."

"Have him hold off till I come back from supper," said the tall man. "I'm so hungry, I could eat a hotel clerk."

The clerk laughed hollowly. "Yessir, Mr. Smith."

Sundeen wheeled and mounted the stairs. The fidgety little man watched Sundeen's broad back until he topped the long flight and disappeared.

Dave entered the room, eased the saddlebags onto an overstuffed chair, and immediately stepped back into the hallway. Locking the door and pocketing the key, he descended the stairs and made his way to the dining room of the hotel. Finding an empty table, he looked around the room as he lowered his long, muscular frame into the chair beside it. Several of the faces were familiar. They had stared at him earlier when he and the sheriff shot it out with the stubborn ruffians.

No sooner had Sundeen given his order to the waitress when a man and woman paused at his table. The man was silver-haired and important-looking. The woman was powdered heavily in a weak attempt at covering her years.

"I want to compliment you on the way you came to our sheriff's aid this afternoon," said the man, offering his hand.

Sundeen rose to his feet.

"I'm Elrod Frame, and this is Mrs. Frame, Mr.—"

"Smith," said Sundeen quickly, "John Smith." He nodded politely at Mrs. Frame as he shook the man's hand.

"I am president of Frame Freight Lines, Mr. Smith," the silver-haired man said with dignity. "Perhaps you noticed our place of business as you rode into town today."

"No, I can't say that I did."

"Well, we're at First and Allen. If I can ever be of service . . ."

"Thank you, Mr. Frame," said Dave, smiling.

As the Frames exited through the door, the waitress placed a cup of steaming coffee in front of the blond man.

By the time he had finished his meal, no less than nine people had paused at Dave's table to express gratitude for his earlier actions on the street. The last to do so was the tall, expensively dressed man to whom he had spoken briefly on the boardwalk just prior to the shootout. He had introduced himself at the table as Bennett Crabtree, president of the Tombstone Bank and Trust Company. He was also chairman of the town council.

As the tall, muscular Sundeen passed through the lobby, he saw a short, stocky Negro with silver hair rise slowly, on aged legs, from a sofa.

"Is you Mistah Smif?" the black man asked pleasantly.

"Yes, sir," replied Dave with a smile. He admired the man's sprightly energy at what Dave judged to be at least seventy years old.

The porter's eyes widened. "Ah's jis da poatah heah, Mistah Smif, you doan need call me *suh*," he said, bending his head low.

Towering over the black man, Sundeen smiled and said, "Yes, sir."

"Mah name is James Louis, Mistah Smif. James Louis Rountree."

Sundeen extended his hand. "Glad to meet you, Mr. Rountree." As their hands met, the older man's face registered astonishment. "It *is* all right if I call you Mister Rountree, isn't it?"

"Well, yassuh," replied Rountree, shaking his head. "It's jist dat ah ain't used to dis kind o' treatment, suh."

"I'm sure that's true, Mr. Rountree. I—"

"Yo' hot watah am ready, Mistah Smif. Ah already put de tub in yo' room. You goes on up an' ah'll fetch up de watah."

"It's a deal, Mr. Rountree," Dave said, moving toward the stairs. He nodded at the mousey clerk as he passed the desk.

Within ten minutes James Louis Rountree had poured the steaming water into the wooden tub. He eyed the rippling muscles of Dave Sundeen, who was stripped to the waist. Hoisting the empty buckets, the porter turned to leave.

"Just a second, Mr. Rountree," said Dave, fishing in his pants pocket. Producing a ten-dollar gold piece, he flipped it toward the aging Negro. Rountree dropped both buckets and caught the coin. As he examined it his eyes widened, then bulged.

"Mistah Smif . . . ah . . . ah ain't got no change," he stammered apprehensively.

"No need," said the tall, muscular man. "It's all yours."

Tears touched the old man's eyes. "Ain't nobody evah gib me no tip like dis, Mistah Smif. Nevah. Nobody!

"Maybe it'll help make up a little," said Dave warmly.

"Ah doan know how to thank yuh, suh."

"Don't have to. You earned it."

"Mistah Smif?"

"Yes."

"We's frien's, raht?"

"Yes."

"Den would you call me *James Louis*? Ah'd feel bettah if'n yo' would."

Sundeen flashed a broad, toothy smile. "Sure. If that's what you want."

"Good night, suh," said the old gentleman, passing through the door, buckets in hand.

"Good night, James Louis."

Dave closed the door and turned the key. He could hear his newfound friend whistling an old spiritual as he walked down the hall. The tune was familiar but he could not recall its name.

The hot water felt good to his travel-weary body. The twin Colts hung on the back of a wooden chair next to the tub. Dave Sundeen had lived too long in the shadow of death to let his guns get more than an arm's reach away. Lawmen west of the Pecos had his picture on file. He was not the kind to hibernate in a cave somewhere, so he had to live with a careful eye over his shoulder.

A greater menace than the law were the bounty hunters. A man with a price on his head was open prey to those grisly predators.

The water had cooled almost to room temperature and he was considering climbing from the tub when there was a light tap on the door.

Instantly one of the revolvers was in his hand. "Who is it?" he bellowed sharply.

The knock was repeated.

"I said, who is it?" Sundeen said even louder.

"Bert Riley," came the answer in a hoarse whisper.

Dave Sundeen's feet made wet marks on the rug as he walked to the door, a towel knotted around his slender waist. Turning the key, he held the gun in one hand and twisted the knob with the other. Opening the door a crack, he peered into the dimly lit hallway.

Riley whispered heavily, "Can I see you a minute?"

"It's not ten o'clock yet," said Dave, not bothering to lower his voice.

"I have a message for you," Riley breathed, an urgency in his words.

"You alone?"

"Yes."

An angular shaft of yellow light filled the hallway briefly as Riley entered the room. Sundeen closed the door and locked it. Walking to the chair and holstering the gun, he said, "What's the message?"

"Mack Evans will be in to see you tomorrow afternoon."

A frown formed on the tall gunslinger's handsome brow. "Why so long?"

"He's working on a job in the morning."

"A job?"

"Yes. A bank job, Mr. Sundeen."

A smile tugged at the corners of Sundeen's mouth. "You know me."

"Yes, sir. Word from Evans was that Dave Sundeen would inquire for him at the Capitol. When you asked for him and I got a gander at you, I knew you had to be Sundeen."

Dave buckled his belt after pulling on a clean pair of pants. "Why do I have to see Evans? Why can't I see the head man?"

"The big boss don't let nobody know who he is until they prove themselves," Riley answered flatly.

"You work for him?" Sundeen asked, putting on a clean shirt.

"In a way," replied Riley. "Sort of a messenger service. My job at the saloon is a perfect setup. Everybody talks to the bartender."

"You've seen the boss this evening?"

"Yes, sir."

"He lives in Tombstone, I take it."

"Uh-huh."

"Prominent citizen?"

"Very."

"Businessman?"

"I can't tell you anymore," Riley said evasively. "Evans will look you up when he comes into town tomorrow afternoon."

"Okay, Riley, but I'm an impatient man. If Mack Evans delays his coming, I'll start turning rocks to find the big man. Understand?"

"I'll pass that on to the boss, sir," the barkeep said shakily.

It was a bright, sunny morning in Benson, Arizona. A soft breeze carried the thin clouds overhead in a southerly direction.

At nine o'clock sharp Seymour Ashley, the cashier of the Benson National Bank, inserted the key in the door and entered the bank. Ashley, a short, portly man of forty-three, was always first to arrive. Marsha Little, the bookkeeper, would be along at about nine fifteen and Myron Mills, the teller, would appear by nine thirty. The bank's president, C. B. Yarrow, would make his usual appearance at nine fifty, the moment set on the timer for the vault to open. Yarrow had almost made a ceremony of the opening of the vault each business day. The new door, complete with automatic timer, had arrived from Kansas City only three weeks earlier. C. B. was like a boy with a new toy.

Promptly at nine fifteen, Miss Little, a skinny spinster in her late fifties, rapped on the window pane of the door. Ashley responded immediately. It was always a special moment for him, when he could use the bank's number two key to open the door for the lesser employees. The only other key was in the pocket of C. B. Yarrow. Ashley felt a tinge of superiority whenever his key unlatched the door for Marsha, but even more so when he admitted Myron Mills. The teller was nine years older than Seymour Ashley, and the latter was adept at keeping the fact fresh in Mills's mind.

True to form, Myron Mills rapped reluctantly at nine thirty.

"Good morning, Mills," Ashley said with a false friendliness.

"Morning," grunted the teller without looking at Ashley. The cashier made a big thing of locking the door behind Mills.

The three employees were busy at their given tasks when C. B. Yarrow opened the door at nine fifty and locked it behind him. Yarrow was a tall, slender man of sixty. His thinning hair was matched by the drooping silver-gray moustache on his upper lip.

The president of Benson National walked promptly to the vault door without greeting his employees. Myron Mills stepped toward the vault. He would need to get his cash drawer.

"Good morning, Mr. Yarrow," said Mills glumly.

"Mmm-hmmm," hummed Yarrow, his full attention on the shiny metal mechanism.

The lock clicked. Smiling to himself, Yarrow pulled the handle on the heavy steel door. As it swung open he said jubilantly, "Ah Mills! Have you ever seen anything like it?"

"No, sir," mumbled the teller as he entered the vault, lifted the cash drawer from a shelf, and headed for his cage.

Immediately Yarrow began to fiddle with the timer.

"Twenty-minute intervals again today, sir?" Seymour Ashley was looking over Yarrow's shoulder.

"Yes, Ashley," the slender banker replied solemnly. "As long as the extra money is in our care, we'll protect it as much as possible. We must be especially cautious with that vile gang hitting banks all over the territory."

"That's for sure, Mr. Yarrow," agreed Ashley. "First Oracle Junction. Then Willcox. We could be next, sir." The cashier's face twisted. "It seems more than coincidence, sir, that the other two banks were robbed when they were holding the San Diego money. Wells Fargo must have someone in the company who is tipping off the robbers about the decoy shipments."

"Must be," concurred Yarrow. "As far as I know, no one has even attempted to rob the stages carrying the empty bags."

"Shouldn't we post some special guards till the money is sent on to San Diego?" asked Ashley.

"Would attract attention," said Yarrow. "We've got to make things look normal. We'll just have to hope that if the gang comes, they'll not want to wait around till the timer releases the lock. Marshal Sellers and the deputy will continue to pass by intermittently."

Business was usual in Smithville. Merchants enjoyed normal activity. The bank was a virtual beehive for the first forty-five minutes of business.

In a deep ravine pocketed in a thick stand of mesquite about a mile west of Benson, Otis Becker eyed the gold watch in his grimy hand. With his other hand he pulled at his beard. "It'll be eleven o'clock if we start right now," he advised his accomplices. "You said the heavy business petered after the first hour, didn't yuh, Mack?"

Mack Evans scratched his thick mop of gray hair and replaced the sweat-stained hat on his big head. "Yep. Did the same thing every day when I watched five days in a row."

All four robbers swung into their respective saddles,

rolls of burlap at their knees. Clinging to Mack Evans's pommel was a large canvas bag.

Smithville lay in the temporary shade of a cloud cluster as Mack Evans, Otis Becker, Neal Furman, and Dick Millard rode quietly down the main street and dismounted in front of Walford's Feed and Supply, which was next door to the bank.

"Looks purty quiet," Becker said, eyeing the bank.

Evans nodded, checking his gun. He handed the large canvas bag to Neal Furman.

Dick Millard trailed a few steps behind the other three as they approached the bank. Their heavy boots made a hollow sound on the board sidewalk. Millard's passionless green eyes swept the street. "Looks good, boys," he said encouragingly. "Go!"

Myron Mills had not had a customer in over ten minutes. He was bundling a stack of one-dollar bills when the hulking frame of Mack Evans charged through the door, followed by Becker and Furman. All three wore bandanna masks.

"Reach for the ceiling!" Evans bellowed.

C. B. Yarrow was just swinging the massive vault door closed. He heard the robbers before he saw them. Swiftly he slammed the door and flipped the handle.

Mack Evans held his gun on the teller, who began filling the small sack provided by the bulky robber. Hurriedly Becker and Furman slipped through the little gate, brandishing Colt .45's.

Furman's dark eyes riveted Seymour Ashley, who sat, terrified, at his desk. His fat frame shook like boiled blubber in an earthquake. "Let's get the big stuff," Furman snapped.

Ashley swallowed hard, eyes bulging, but could not find his voice.

Becker cast a fleeting look at the frail woman who

sat before a table stacked with ledgers. She was frozen with fright. C. B. Yarrow stood by the vault, a fearless, obstinate look on his wrinkled face.

"We want the Wells Fargo money. Open the vault," commanded the heavy-set Becker.

A malevolent grin curled the banker's thin lips. "Then sit down, sir," Yarrow said with cool control. "You'll have a thirty-minute wait."

Furman forsook the terrified cashier and lunged for Yarrow. Jamming the muzzle of his .45 into the slender man's flat stomach, he hissed, "Open the vault this instant, pops, or you're a dead man!"

The bank president looked down his long nose at the partially visible, swarthy face of Neal Furman. "Impossible," he said flatly. "This door is on a timer. It has thirty minutes to go."

Furman flashed a look toward the teller's cage, where Mack Evans was watching Myron Mills stuff money into the small sack. "Hey! This joker says there's a timer on the vault door. You never said anything about it!"

Evans stepped away from the cage, cast a quick glance at the front door, and set his attention on Furman. "He's lyin'. Make him open it!" hooted Evans.

Furman reacted by shoving the muzzle hard into Yarrow's stomach. "Open it or I'll spill your guts on the floor."

"I'm telling you the truth," insisted Yarrow, gritting his teeth in pain.

Otis Becker stepped to the vault door. "Where's the timer?" he asked Yarrow.

The tall, slender man swallowed hard. "In that metal box."

Becker swung open the lid on the box attached to the vault door. Squinting momentarily, he studied the clock inside.

"He ain't lyin' about the timer," he hollered to Evans. Turning to face Yarrow with fire in his eyes, he added loudly, "But he lied about the time. It's got nineteen minutes to go."

Mack Evans jerked the swollen sack from the teller's fingers. "You lie down on the floor," he ordered Mills. Looking through the bars to Marsha Little, he snapped, "You too, sister!" Both immediately complied.

Evans charged toward the vault like an angry bull. As he kneed open the double-hinged gate, he flashed Seymour Ashley a hard look. "You get on the floor too, porky!"

Ashley, his face pallid, melted quietly to the floor.

The hulking outlaw stepped to the little metal box and scrutinized its contents. A violent oath escaped his thick lips.

At the same moment Dick Millard dashed through the front door, pulling the bandanna over his nose. "What's the delay in here?" he demanded.

"There's a timer on the vault," Otis Becker announced heavily. "Got eighteen minutes to go."

Millard cursed. "The town marshal and his deputy just rode by. I tried to look innocent, but they examined me mighty close. I got a feelin' they'll be back shortly, maybe with help. We better light a shuck outta here!"

"I hate to go without that hunnerd thousand!" said Evans sourly.

"If we wait that long, they could have the whole town recruited," Millard lashed back.

"He's right," agreed Becker. "We'd better git."

A triumphant smile spread across C. B. Yarrow's face. Mack Evans, temper hot, swung his revolver in a wide arc, connecting with Yarrow's left temple. He went down like an axed sapling. In his fury Evans cursed and said, "If we can't get it, I'll make it tough for everybody." With that, he smashed the clock in the metal box to smithereens.

Within one minute the fearsome four were safely out of town.

CHAPTER TWELVE

Bright morning sunshine filled Dave Sundeen's hotel room as he dried his freshly shaven face. He ran a comb through his coarse hair and fluffed his heavy moustache, which matched the color of his blond locks. Tucking his shirt under his belt, he donned the twin Colts and tied the leather thongs to his sinewy thighs.

Placing the Stetson at a slight angle on his head, he unlocked and opened the door, ducked beneath the lintel, and headed for the dining room. The tantalizing smell of hot breakfast met his nostrils as he descended the stairs.

James Louis Rountree was just entering the lobby door from the boardwalk, broom in hand. "Moanin', Mistah Smif," he said cheerfully, exposing a mouthful of white teeth, which were accentuated by his dark skin.

"Good morning, James Louis," said Sundeen, returning the smile. "Have you had breakfast?"

"Yassah, ah took care o' James Louis's innah man 'bout a houah ago."

"Okay. See you later," said the tall man as he stepped toward the pleasant-smelling dining room.

Dave was just finishing his breakfast of steak, eggs, potatoes, muffins, and coffee when four men entered the room. He recognized three of them. Bennett Crabtree was in the lead, followed by Roy Teal. Next was a middle-aged man with thin sandy hair and a ruddy face whom Dave had not met. Bringing up the rear was Elrod Frame.

The tall, well-built Crabtree headed straight for Sundeen's table. The others followed.

"Good morning, Mr. Smith," said Crabtree, sporting a wide smile. "Could we talk to you for a moment?"

Dave wiped his mouth with a napkin. "Certainly," he said cordially. Gesturing toward the other three chairs, he said, "Sit down, gentlemen."

Teal, the red-faced man, and Elrod Frame slacked into the three chairs. Crabtree took a chair from another table and swung it next to Frame, where he could face Sundeen.

"I believe you've met Roy Teal of the Capitol?" asked the banker.

"Yes," replied Dave, nodding at Teal.

"You know Elrod Frame of Frame Freight Lines, I believe."

"Yes," said Sundeen, acknowledging the silver-haired man.

"I don't think you've met Al Pierce, editor of the Tombstone *Epitaph*."

"No, but it's my pleasure," said Dave, lifting slightly out of his chair and shaking Pierce's hand.

Bennett Crabtree cleared his throat. "We have a proposition for you, Mr. Smith. Doc Freeman says that Sheriff Springer is going to be out of commission for a couple of months. It would be even longer if it had been his other shoulder."

Dave Sundeen dipped his chin, knowing what was coming. His sky-blue eyes remained fixed on Crabtree's face.

"As the town council of Tombstone, we have authority from the county to hire an acting sheriff if the elected man cannot function. We like the way you handle yourself. We are prepared to offer you a hundred and fifty dollars a month plus hotel and eating expenses if you'll take the job."

Sundeen was silent for a long moment. He wondered what they would say if they knew there was a price on his head. He had come to Tombstone to join up with a gang of bank robbers. A big heist was pending in Tucson, one that could net him at least a hundred thousand dollars. He certainly would not need the three hundred that a couple of months' sheriff pay would produce. Besides, wearing a badge would be totally out of character for Dave Sundeen, the outlaw.

"Aren't there a couple of deputies?" asked Dave, evading the issue.

"They're too young and inexperienced," interjected Elrod Frame. "We need a man like you. Tombstone is a tough town."

"How about it?" asked Crabtree.

Sundeen started to voice a flat refusal when the thought crossed his mind that he did not know how soon the Tucson job would be pulled off. If it were not right away, the job as acting sheriff would make a good coverup for his presence in Tombstone.

"Give me till tomorrow morning," said the tall man in a congenial tone. "I've got some business to tend to today. When I'm finished I'll have a better picture of my present situation. Then I'll know whether I can be available for the job."

"That will be fine unless trouble develops between now and tomorrow morning," said Crabtree listlessly.

"Well, Bennett, look at it this way," said Roy Teal. "If Smith, here, hadn't come to Tombstone, Springer would be dead and we wouldn't even have a prospect for a new man."

Crabtree nodded. "You're right, Roy. We'll just have

to tough it out till tomorrow." Looking at Sundeen, he said, "Sure hope you'll give us an affirmative answer tomorrow, Smith."

"We'll see," said Dave with a tight grin.

The four Tombstone leaders left quietly. Dave ordered another cup of coffee.

It was nearly nine o'clock when Dave Sundeen walked through the lobby and stepped out on the board sidewalk. He had half a day to kill before Mack Evans was to show up. He was pondering his course of action when he heard the sound of a ruckus from around the corner of the building. Figuring it was none of his business, he turned the other way and started down the boardwalk.

Suddenly a hoarse voice guffawed and he heard the word "nigger," followed by dissolute laughter. The only black man he had seen in Tombstone was James Louis Rountree.

Wheeling, he made for the side of the Arizona Hotel. Rounding the corner, he saw two saddle tramps holding Rountree on the ground facedown next to a rainbarrel, which was half-full of water. An empty wooden bucket lay on its side in the dust. One of the men was pushing the old man's face in the dirt, saying, "Eat it, nigger! Eat it!"

Dave Sundeen's hair-trigger temper burst into flame. Before either saddle tramp saw him, his boot caught the one holding Rountree's legs square in the mouth. He keeled over like a slaughtered steer.

Arms like tempered steel lifted the second man into midair and slammed him savagely to the ground. He rolled over, his face contorted with pain. As he rose to his knees, Sundeen's muscular knee slammed his nose with vehement force. Leaving him to spit blood and writhe in the dust, Dave tenderly lifted James Louis to his feet. As he did so, he noted that the first man was unconscious.

BOOT HILL BROTHER

The elderly Negro steadied himself by flattening his palms against the wall of the hotel.

Sundeen returned to the man whose nose was spewing blood. Cursing the tall man, he was on his knees again, clawing for his gun. Sundeen's foot flashed forward, thumping him in the stomach. He buckled forward and went white with pain. Dave reached down and lifted the man's gun from its holster and tossed it into the rainbarrel. Only then did he notice that he had gained an audience of about two dozen men and women.

Flashing a quick look at the first man, he saw him beginning to stir. Dave was sure he had kicked out all of his front teeth. He relieved this one of his gun also. Dropping it in the barrel with a splash, he returned to the man with the caved-in stomach, who was on his feet, sucking air.

Sundeen approached him, locked his foot behind one heel, and tripped him. The man hit the ground hard. Sundeen was immediately on top of him, holding him belly down. Filling his fist with hair, Dave pushed his bleeding face in the dirt. "Eat it, scum!" he hissed. "Eat it!"

The saddle tramp wept like a child while he lapped dust with his tongue. The gathering crowd began to cheer.

Sundeen jerked him to his feet and held him by his shirt collar. The man stumbled helplessly as Dave dragged him toward his comrade, who was looking on in horror. Grasping the horrified man's collar, he marched them both to where the elderly Rountree stood leaning against the wall.

"Now you two hunks of coyote meat tell Mr. Rountree you're sorry!" the angry man said through clenched teeth.

Neither man spoke. Dave snapped their necks violently. A woman in the crowd ejected a weak gasp.

"I—I'm sorry," mumbled the man with the broken front teeth.

"Me too," said the other with cold reluctance.

Releasing the other man, Sundeen slapped and backhanded him fiercely several times. "You tell him you're sorry that you called him a nigger."

Half choking, the saddle tramp said, "I'm sorry I called you a nigger."

"Tell him you ate the dirt for him."

"I—I ate the dirt for you."

Again the crowd cheered and broke into applause.

Eyeing both beaten men, Dave Sundeen said, "Can you two find your way out of town?"

"Y—yes," one gasped.

"Then hop to it. If you're not gone in three minutes, I'll kill you both. Understand?"

The crowd parted, allowing the frightened men to pass through and stumble to their horses. In less than a minute they were gone.

It was nearly sundown when Mack Evans parted the batwings of the Capitol Saloon. Slapping a coin on the bar, he loudly ordered a drink. Bert Riley leaned close so that only Evans could hear. "Sundeen is at the Arizona. Room three. He's probably chomping at the bit by now. He has a thin thread on his temper. You'd best get on over there."

"I had to stop and see the boss first," Evans retorted defensively. "Sundeen is gonna want to know about the Tucson job. I wanted to get the latest word from the boss first."

The big man downed a glass of whiskey, poured it full, and downed another. He was pouring the third one when Riley said, "You upset about something?"

"Hit a snag at Benson today. Boss had me scout out the bank a couple weeks ago. Stupid bank had one of them newfangled timers installed. I didn't know it. We didn't get the Wells Fargo money. Only nine thousand from the cage."

Tossing down the third belt, Evans added, "Boss just reamed me out royally." He banged the glass on the bar hard enough to attract attention from all over the room. "See you later," he said to Riley. His massive frame nearly tore the batwings off the doorframe as he charged through them angrily.

Five minutes later the formidable Evans knocked on Dave Sundeen's door. Footsteps sounded from within. A deep voice said, "Who is it?"

"Mack Evans," the two-hundred-and-sixty-pound giant roared.

The lock made a rattling noise, the knob turned, and the door opened.

Dave Sundeen was two inches taller than the six-foot-one-inch Evans. The heavier man looked up at the tall man with the pale blue eyes. "Sundeen?"

"Come in," said Dave, throwing open the door.

Evans entered the room. It seemed to shrink in size.

"Sit down," offered Sundeen, motioning toward the overstuffed chair. "You get my wire?"

"The boss did," answered Evans. "Telegraph operator knows me and the boss are friends."

As Evans eased himself into the chair, Dave swung the straight-backed wooden chair from its place by the window and sat down, straddling it with the back side forward. As he fixed his gaze on the big man, Evans spoke.

"We're gonna have a short delay on the Tucson job. Indian trouble over in Colorado has made it necessary to run the shipment in a wider circle. Gonna take at least a couple more weeks. Boss said to give you some advance money." Pulling a thick roll of bills from his pocket, he said, "Couple hundred do?"

"I'm in good shape," said Dave, throwing his palms up. "I can wait."

"Whatever you say," retorted Evans, shrugging his huge shoulders and pocketing the roll.

"When do I meet the boss?" asked Sundeen impatiently.

"Probably just before we pull the job," said Evans, crossing his thick legs. "He wants to make sure you're made out of the right stuff."

"Eddie Dalton told him I was all right or he wouldn't have asked me to come."

"The boss has no doubts as to your ability with those two hoglegs on your hips. Dalton told him you were fast . . . and cool as an iceberg in a shootout." Evans chuckled. "Boss saw you prove that yesterday."

"He was in the crowd when the sheriff and I shot it out with those mangy curs yesterday?"

Evans nodded silently. "He's watching you. It's not your ability he's concerned about. It's your *dependability*. He wants to make sure you're our kind. When he is convinced, you'll know it. He'll reveal himself to you."

Dave thought of the offer made by the town council. The big boss might question his "kind" if he were to pin on a badge. However, the brief stint as acting sheriff offered him a challenge never before experienced. After all, with the delay in the Tucson job, it would present a good excuse for his stay in Tombstone.

"How long would it take you to carry a message to your boss and bring me back an answer?" Dave asked, rocking his chair on two legs.

"I can be back in half an hour," said Evans, uncrossing his legs.

"Tell him the town council wants me to wear the star while John Springer is recuperating. It would give me a good front while I'm waiting for Wells Fargo to get the half-million dollars to Tucson."

Evans smiled as he lifted his big frame out of the chair.

"I have to give them an answer in the morning," Dave said, rising to his feet.

"I'll be back in half an hour," said Mack Evans, stepping toward the door. Eyeing Sundeen warily, he said, "You wouldn't try to follow me?"

"Nope. I'm willing to let the hotshot play his little game. I'll put up with a lot for a hundred thousand simoleons."

Evans pulled open the door.

"That *is* to be the amount of my cut, isn't it?" asked Dave with his blue eyes narrowed.

"Yep," said Evans. "That's what the boss told Eddie to tell you."

"Good. See you in half an hour."

Within twenty minutes Mack Evans was knocking on Sundeen's door again. As the huge man passed through the door, he said, "Boss already knew about the offer. Says it's a good idea. But just one thing . . ."

"What's that?"

"He said don't get yourself killed sheriffin'. He needs you for the Tucson job."

CHAPTER THIRTEEN

Sheriff John Springer lived at the Purple Sage Hotel, at Third and Fremont. He had come to Tombstone as sheriff only thirteen months before. The county voters had decided that new blood in the sheriff's office was healthy. They also felt that a stranger to the territory would be less apt to show bias toward local lawbreakers. At least this was the strength of Springer's platform during the election.

Tombstone's incumbent sheriff was over sixty. His gun hand had slowed and he had shown less desire to handle troublemakers properly. Springer had served for some time as a town marshal in Texas. He was approaching forty. His forceful personality and comparative youth had garnered the heavy vote.

Bennett Crabtree and Dave Sundeen walked the two blocks from the Arizona to the Purple Sage in the midmorning sunshine. "John is sitting up and taking nourishment this morning, Mr. Smith," said Crabtree. "I have a badge here in my pocket. He can swear you in. Both deputies are to meet us at John's room."

Crabtree knocked on Springer's door. A matronly woman opened it. Smiling at the banker, she said, "Come in, Mr. Crabtree."

"Mrs. Rowland, this is John Smith," said Crabtree. "He is going to be our acting sheriff until Mr. Springer recuperates."

"Pleased to meet you, sir," smiled the gray-headed woman.

Dave touched the brim of his hat. "My pleasure, ma'am."

John Springer was propped up on the bed, his left arm in a sling. A broad smile spread across his mouth as his dark brown eyes fell on Sundeen's face. "I woke up to good news this morning, friend," he said. "Bennett came by right after the two of you talked earlier." Extending his right hand slowly and laboriously, he added, "How can I thank you for cutting in with me? I'd be dead if you hadn't."

"Don't need to thank me," said Sundeen, squeezing Springer's hand. "Couldn't just stand there and let you go it alone." His blue gaze caught Crabtree's eye. The banker quickly looked away.

"Stine and Pardee will show you the ropes," said Springer. "They'll take care of all the paperwork and such. All you need worry about is just keeping the peace."

Sundeen nodded.

"Let's get you sworn in," Springer said, tossing a glance at Bennett Crabtree. Looking Dave in the eye, he said, "Raise your right hand."

Sundeen complied.

"Do you promise to uphold the law as acting sheriff of this county to the best of your knowledge and ability?"

"I do."

"Give him the badge, Bennett," Springer said, smiling.

Dave accepted the badge and pinned it to his leather vest.

There was a light rap at the door. Mrs. Rowland waddled to the door and pulled it open. Looking past her, Springer saw the two deputies. "Come in, boys!"

he said warmly. "Shake hands with . . . *Dave Sundeen.*"

The tall man wheeled to face John Springer, his eyes wide.

"I knew who you were the minute I got a good look at your face when I was lying in the dirt the day before yesterday. Have a picture of you over at the office."

Dave ran his hand over his mouth, brushing his moustache. "You know I'm wanted in Texas . . . and you still put this badge on me?"

"As I recall, it's more Arizona than Texas now. You shot up some lawman over in Holbrook and the big thing is your escape from Yuma."

A quizzical look twisted Sundeen's handsome face. "I put a bullet in Holbrook's marshal to slow him down. But I've never been in Yuma Territorial Prison."

Springer snickered in disbelief. "All this talk doesn't mean a thing, Sundeen. You put your own life on the line to save my hide. As far as I know . . . or anybody else in this town knows, Dave Sundeen could be the next president of the United States and Territories."

Looking at the faces in the room, Sundeen said, "What about these four?"

"Mrs. Rowland has a steel clamp on her jaw. Bennett, here, has his whole life invested in this town. All he's interested in is seeing it protected."

"Right," said the banker flatly.

"Ralph Stine and Slim Pardee both know they're too green to be the number one lawman in Tombstone."

"That's right," spoke up Stine, the short stocky deputy. "I'm mighty glad to have you at the helm, Mr. Sundeen."

"Yeah," chimed in the tall, lanky Pardee. "Me too."

Sundeen smiled and shook their hands.

After a brief discourse on Dave's duties as sheriff, Springer said, "If you have any questions the boys can't answer, you know where to find me."

"Thanks," said Dave, lifting his hat, running his fingers through his hair, and replacing the hat.

The deputies left first, followed by Bennett Crabtree, who said he had business at the bank.

As Sundeen started to close the door behind him, Springer said, "Sundeen . . . thanks again . . . for my life."

Several days passed in Tombstone with no more trouble than a couple of drunks requiring tossing in the jail to sleep it off overnight, and a few fights in the saloons.

On the morning of the eleventh day, Sheriff Dave Sundeen was leaving Hurley's Gun Shop, carrying a sack bearing several boxes of forty-five caliber bullets. As he pulled the door closed, a flash of sunlight from the star on his chest caught his eye. *I'll never get used to this lawman stuff*, he thought. *Too many years on the other side.* He felt like a fish out of water.

Stepping off the boardwalk and angling across the street toward the sheriff's office, Dave was convincing himself that this brief chapter in his life as a lawman would be worth it when he held that hundred thousand dollars in his hands.

His thinking drifted to the mysterious leader of the outlaw gang who was successfully masquerading as one of Tombstone's citizens. Deep in his thoughts, the tall man did not notice the two unshaven riders draw abreast and slowly pass. About the time he reached the boardwalk on the other side, one of the riders jerked on the reins and wheeled his mount. "Well, I'll be a suck-egg mule!" he shouted. "If it ain't Dave Sundeen!"

Dave turned to face the man as he approached on the horse. Sighting in on his face, the tall man drew a blank.

"Why, you old sidewinder," the unfamiliar character said, shaking his head, "am I seein' things? Now that ain't no sheriff's badge you got tacked on yore chest!"

The loudmouth's partner had now reined beside him, eyeing Dave Sundeen pretentiously.

"Hey, Hecky, I want you to meet my old prisonmate! Dave Sundeen! And looky, looky. He's done got religion and put on a badge!"

Sundeen held his face expressionless. From the corner of his eye he saw townspeople gawking at the boisterous stranger. Directly across the street stood James Louis Rountree holding a large paper bag, eyes wide.

"I don't know you, mister," Dave said evenly. "I have no idea how you know my name, but I'm not anybody's old prisonmate."

"Aw, c'mon, Dave. Arlie Skinner . . . you know! Yuma? Now you're not gonna tell me you didn't do a stretch in Yuma and wrangle yourself an easy escape when the whole place come down with cholera?"

Skinner turned his head slightly, keeping his eyes on Sundeen, and spat a stream of brown juice in the street.

Anger was beginning to surface with Dave Sundeen. Suddenly the words spoken by John Springer the day Dave was sworn in reverberated in his mind: "As I recall, it's more Arizona than Texas now. You shot up some lawman over in Holbrook *and the big thing is your escape from Yuma.*"

Dave's mind was spinning, searching for an explanation, when the grating voice of Arlie Skinner cut into his thoughts. "Hey, boy, I owe you one, remember?"

"You what?" Dave queried blankly.

"You know . . . that day at the water tank, when I was just funnin' and said somethin' about your dead friend, Pete Linwood. You belted me in the chops, remember?"

Sundeen's brain seemed to freeze. His pale blue eyes bolted Skinner with anger.

"I swore I'd get you for it, old pal . . . but I'll tell you what. I'm willin' to let bygones be bygones if you promise to stay outta my way while I'm in this jerkwater town. Just wanta have me a little fun, okay?"

Dave's head cleared momentarily. The anger was running hot in his veins, like water about to become steam. "You came from the south, right?" Dave asked heatedly.

"Yep," retorted Skinner, spitting again.

"Just keep heading north."

"Now looky here, old pal," said Skinner with a veneer of innocence, "me and my partner, here, have been on the trail for days. We done worked ourselves up a frightful dry thirst."

Dave noted that James Louis Rountree had crossed the street and was standing less than ten feet away. Next to him were deputies Stine and Pardee.

Tombstone's acting sheriff squared his jaw, pointed to a nearby water trough, and said, "You two can quench your thirst right there . . . that is, unless the horses object to drinking after you."

The gunfighter instinct imbedded deeply in Dave Sundeen's nature flashed the message to his reflexes a split second before Arlie Skinner clawed for his gun. Before Skinner's fingers could close on the grips, the muzzle of Sundeen's right-hand Colt was staring at him like a threatening eye. "You're lucky I'm not in a killing mood, *old pal*," Dave said calmly.

The ex-convict's hand remained close to the gun-butt. Sundeen said from the side of his mouth, "Ralph, get his gun. Rifle too. Slim, you get his partner's." As the deputies complied, the tall man wearing the sheriff's star said, "You boys escort these two coyotes to the north end of town. Empty their guns and give 'em back. Make sure they keep on riding."

Skinner flinched as Ralph Stine relieved him of his guns. Pardee mounted his horse, carrying Hecky's guns. Stine boarded his mount and motioned the two outlaws northward.

Arlie Skinner's face was livid with rage. Sullenly he rode away with his partner, followed by Stine and Pardee.

As Dave Sundeen holstered the .45, his gaze swept over the crowd. He read suspicion in their eyes. Edging toward the boardwalk, he faced James Louis Rountree.

"Mistah Smif," he said tenderly, "ah doan care if'n you was in prison, ah's still yo' frien'."

"James Louis, I told you my name is *Sundeen*. Smith was only an alias," Dave said kindly.

"Ah keeps fohgettin'," said Rountree apologetically.

"And the man lied," said Sundeen in an even tone. "I've never been in Yuma Prison."

"Ah would be yo' frien' even if yo' *was* a outlaw," said the old man, showing his mouthful of white teeth.

Dave squeezed his shoulder. "And I'd be your friend even if *you* were an outlaw," he chuckled.

As the tall blond man walked toward the sheriff's office, a sense of dread washed over him. Springer's earlier remark about Yuma had not taken effect until now. One thing was for sure: Dave Sundeen had to see the "wanted" poster in Springer's file.

Looking up, he spied John Springer standing just outside the office door, waiting for him.

"How's the shoulder today?" Dave asked with interest.

"Better than yesterday," answered Springer, adjusting the sling. "I'm able to ride again. Just got back, in fact," he said, pointing to his horse at the hitchrail. "What was that all about?"

"I think my marbles need rearranging," said Dave, shaking his head. "The ugliest of those two honyocks said he'd been in Yuma Prison with me."

"So?"

"John, I've never been in Yuma Prison."

"What are you talking about?" asked Springer, shifting his broad shoulders. "Your poster says—"

"Yeah . . . I want to see that poster." Ducking his head and shouldering through the door, he pulled open a file drawer.

"It'll be under number two," advised Springer, following.

"Number two?" said Dave, flipping dividers.

"Yes. Number one is for murderers, rapists, torture experts . . . the real bad ones. Number two is for robbers, thieves, embezzlers, and the like."

In seconds Dave produced the poster. It was a perfect artist's sketch of his face. There it was in bold print: He was wanted in El Paso and Fort Worth for bank and stagecoach robbery. He was wanted in Arizona Territory for assaulting a law officer and escaping from Arizona territorial prison at Yuma.

"Impossible." The word fell from his lips automatically.

"Hey, you're really serious," said Springer, eyeing Sundeen carefully.

"Like a case of consumption," Dave said humorlessly.

"You've really never been in that prison?"

"No."

"Well, that hardcase just made a mistake in identity," said Springer reassuringly. "He's got you mixed up with someone else."

"It wasn't just my face, John. *He knew my name.*"

John Springer left Dave to his bewilderment, explaining that the ride had sapped his strength.

Sundeen thought of the general attitude of distrust conveyed by the townspeople after Arlie Skinner's outburst. *That shipment had better arrive in Tucson soon,* he thought. *This outlaw's masquerade as a lawman is about to terminate.*

Dave decided he should contact Mack Evans and see if the big boss had any late word from his source of information in the Wells Fargo organization. As always, he had to work through Bert Riley to see Evans.

As Sundeen made his way up the street toward the Capitol Saloon under the suspicious eyes of passersby, he went over the roster in his mind. For nearly two weeks he had tried to determine who the boss of the gang might be. By remaining anonymous, the man could maintain his position in Tombstone, which possibly was his link to Wells Fargo information. Otherwise, why didn't he just jump in whole hog and run the gang? On the other hand he may be the kind that doesn't want to dirty his hands. Maybe he was tipped off on the secret money shipments by some traitor within the Wells Fargo ranks. *One thing is for certain,* Dave reasoned: *The guilty man is the only one with the link to the information. The link is his leverage, used to wrangle others to do the dirty work while he takes a healthy slice of the loot.*

Dave Sundeen considered the possibilities. *Bennett Crabtree?* Dave shook his head. Certainly it was not likely that a bank president would involve himself in such nefarious activities. He would be risking a successful career. However, Dave had to remind himself that men will do a lot of things for money. He thought of his own guilt in that matter.

Elrod Frame? In a sense Wells Fargo was a competitor. They did handle freight. Frame certainly was a good suspect.

BOOT HILL BROTHER 163

Roy Teal? Certainly a good many saloon owners had been known to dip their fingers into lawless ventures.

Al Pierce? Maybe.

Hubert Farley, the town barber? Hardly. Yes, but possibly.

As Dave Sundeen passed the Arizona Hotel, James Louis Rountree lifted himself from a bench by the lobby door. The tall man paused, recognizing the old man's presence. Rountree's eyes were wide.

"Mistah Smi—ah mean, Mistah Sundeen, ah sho' doan like da way some people am talkin'."

"About me, you mean?"

"Yassuh. Aftah whut dat mangy skunk said 'bout you bein' in prison, folks sayin' you shouldn't be a wearin' dat badge. Ah bin tellin' 'em dat it was a lie. Dat you is mah frien' an' you tole me it was a lie."

Sundeen patted Rountree's shoulder. "I appreciate your sticking up for me, James Louis."

"You did moah dan stick up fo' me whin dem fellas wuz makin' me eat dirt," Rountree said warmly.

"Only did what a man oughtta do," replied Dave.

"Dat's whut ah is doin' too!" said James Louis, nodding his head doggedly.

Dave smiled thinly. "I'll see you a little later."

Rountree nodded.

Sundeen proceeded toward the saloon, his boots making a hollow sound, his spurs jingling.

Maybe Bert Riley is the big boss, Dave thought as he looked at the bartender's face. *Sure would be possible.*

"What'll it be?" asked Riley in a friendly tone.

"I need to see Mack Evans," Dave said tightly. "This badge is getting heavy. I need to know about that Tucson job."

"Yeah, I heard about the ruckus in the street. Talk ain't too favorable toward you right now."

"Evans . . ." Impatience showed in Sundeen's face.

"He oughtta be showin' up around sundown. I'll tell him to shake a leg over to the office," Riley said nervously.

"You do that," said Sundeen.

Bert Riley followed Dave Sundeen's broad back with hard eyes as the towering man moved toward the door and passed through the batwings.

CHAPTER FOURTEEN

The gray of evening was settling on the desert as Mack Evans rode into Tombstone. Soft yellow lights were beginning to appear in the houses.

Dave Sundeen was touching a match to the wick of a lantern in the sheriff's office when the massive Evans dismounted at the hitchrail. Both deputies had gone home.

"I got good news for you," Evans said with a toothy smile, his huge frame filling the door.

"Good, I can use it," replied the handsome blond man.

"The Fargo shipment is in Tucson at the First National Bank. Half a million."

"So what's the plan?"

"We're to meet at the hideout at midnight. I'll take you there."

"The big boss gonna be there?"

"Yes."

"It's about time."

Evans scratched his beard and then his ribs.

"There's a cure for that," said Sundeen dryly.

"For whut?"

"All that itching."

"Yeah?"

"It's called *bathing*."

Ignoring Dave's remark, the formidable Evans said, "I'm gonna meet with the boss up till about eleven o'clock. Get the details worked out. He'll ride ahead of us. Be there when we arrive."

"Why doesn't he just ride with us?" Dave asked with furrowed brow.

"Boss has his own way of doing things," said Evans, turning to leave. "Will you be here or at the hotel?"

"I'll meet you at the livery. Ten after eleven. Okay?"

"Good enough," replied Evans, stepping out into the near-darkness.

Dave sat behind the desk and heaved a sigh of relief. He was glad the brief tenure of acting sheriff was about over. Especially in the light of today's events.

It was exactly midnight as Mack Evans and Dave Sundeen rode up to the old ranch house. The door was open, casting a square of light out into the darkness. As the two men dismounted in the moonless gloom, a bulky shadow filled the door, gun in hand.

"Jackrabbit," said Mack Evans casually.

"C'mon in, Mack," said a gravelly voice.

As Dave followed Evans into the house, his eyes immediately shot to the faces of the three men who lurked in the dim light of the single lantern. Not one was familiar. The room reeked with the odor of tobacco, whiskey, sweat, and dirty bodies.

"Want you fellas to shake hands with Dave Sundeen," said Evans, gesturing toward the tall, broad-shouldered man who wore the twin Colts.

Pointing to a thick-bodied man, he said, "This here is Otis Becker." Dave recognized his form as the one that had filled the doorway a moment earlier.

"Howdy, Sundeen," said Becker, extending his hand.

"And this is Dick Millard."

Dave shook hands with the slender outlaw, noting the cold green eyes set in a narrow face. Millard smiled meagerly. "Glad to meet you, Sundeen. I've been hearin' a lot about your fast draw."

Sundeen made no comment.

"And this," continued Evans, "is Neal Furman."

Furman's long black hair shook as he pumped Sundeen's hand. "Howdy," he said pleasantly.

Sundeen looked around expectantly, twisting his head both ways. "Isn't somebody missing?" he asked, filtering a slight note of irritation into his voice.

"Nope," rasped Becker.

"I'm talking about the boss," said Dave impatiently.

"He's here," said Furman, pointing toward the dark hallway that led to the two bedrooms.

Casting a glance in that direction, Dave saw an obscure form seated in a chair in the darkness. The face was totally indistinct.

The man spoke in a hoarse whisper. It was an obvious effort to disguise his voice. "Explain the situation to him, Mack."

"Now look here," said Sundeen querulously, "I've had about enough of this cat-and-mouse stuff."

"The boss thinks it best to keep things the way they are until the job is finished," said the huge Mack Evans.

Sundeen's back stiffened. "I don't see why—"

"What do you care as long as you walk away with a hundred thousand dollars?" asked Becker. "That's more than us four are gonna make. Boss is gonna put up fifty thousand outta his half. We're gonna put up the other. That leaves us with fifty each."

"How come you're all so quick to cut me in?" asked Dave, looking toward the dark hallway.

"We need your cool manner in the face of gun muzzles . . . and your expert use of *two* guns almost gives us another man," came the veiled voice.

Hunching his shoulders and letting them drop in resignation, the tall man said, "Okay, let's get on with it."

Circling around the table, the motley group and

Dave Sundeen sat down in full view of the man in the shadows.

"The half-million is for the railroad payroll," said Mack Evans. "They've put on several hunnerd extra men to close the gap between Albuquerque and Phoenix. Indian trouble has slowed down the progress of laying track. Wells Fargo plans to have the money in Phoenix in five days. This will be just about two days before the last section of track is laid."

"What kind of protection they gonna have?" asked Dave.

"Army," replied Evans. "Boss says they'll send six cavalrymen from Fort Chandler to escort the Wells Fargo officials who are accompanying the money. The bank in Tucson will not release the money until the cavalrymen arrive and are ready for the trip."

"That's why we wanted you along," chimed Otis Becker. "Takin' out six professional soldiers could get sticky."

"Where do you plan to hit them?" queried Sundeen.

"Half-Moon Pass," said Mack Evans. "North of Tucson about twelve miles. It's perfect for total surprise. Rock formations are good there. The narrow passageway is in the curved shape of a half-moon."

Sundeen cast a careless glance at the hallway as the boss changed positions.

"We figger to plant these three boys up in the rocks with rifles, and you and me will jump in front of 'em in the passageway," continued Evans. "If they start trouble, the boys in the rocks can open fire."

Sundeen tilted the Stetson to the back of his head, rocked the chair on its rear legs, and folded his arms across his chest. "When I set up a robbery, I want the least possible risk of shooting. Don't bother me to kill a man who has challenged me to a shootout, but killing someone I'm stealing from is something else."

"You got a better plan?" breathed the boss.

Looking toward the hallway, Dave said, "Yep."

"I'm listening."

"Instead of jumping them *after* they go to Tucson, why not jump them *before*? Get the drop on them and take their mounts and uniforms. We could tie up five of them and leave one man to guard them. Take their leader to insure getting the money out of the bank."

"I'm still listening," said the deceptive voice.

"They'll be less apt to put up a fight if they don't have the Wells Fargo men and money to protect."

"You're making sense, Sundeen. Go ahead," said the boss.

"The army officer will be in a pinch to cooperate with us. We'll tell him if he blows it, his men die."

"That'll work, boss," said Mack Evans emphatically. "No officer would let his men be killed over money."

"There's only one hitch in this here scheme," spoke up Otis Becker, who was building a cigarette. "If we're gonna masquerade as soldiers, we'll have to shave and get haircuts."

"And bathe," added Sundeen.

Neal Furman picked up a whiskey bottle off the table and pulled out the cork. "I ain't gittin' no haircut," he said heavily, putting the bottle to his lips.

"Not for fifty thousand dollars?" asked Dick Millard.

"Sure he will," came the hoarse whisper from the murky hallway. "I like the plan, Sundeen. Mack will be the one to stay with the hostages. He's big and he's mean. The officer will cooperate when he knows Mack's gonna be with his men. Besides . . . it'd be mighty rare to find a U.S. Army man as big as him. He couldn't get into a uniform."

"Right, boss," chuckled Evans, his eyes meeting Furman's haughtily.

Neal Furman swallowed a mouthful of liquor, slammed the bottle on the table, and cursed. "I said I ain't gonna git no haircut!"

"You'll do what the boss says, Neal," sliced Evans indignantly.

"I liked the first plan best," rasped Furman, his dark eyes flashing. "It's the first plan or count me out!" he said, jumping to his feet.

Sundeen lowered his uptilted chair to the floor. Evans leaned forward and looked Furman in the eye.

"Look, mister," hissed Evans, "I got you this job and you're gonna cooperate, understand?"

Defiance leaped to Furman's eyes. He started to speak when Evans's big fist caught him flush on the jaw. Furman's head snapped back savagely. He slammed against the wall eight feet away and slid to a sitting position. He was out cold.

Mack Evans walked across the room to where his own saddlebags lay. He produced a long-bladed hunting knife. The others watched with interest as the huge man cut great handfuls of hair from the unconscious man's head.

"When he wakes up and gets a gander at himself in that mirror on the wall," said Evans, "he'll be glad to go to the barbershop."

"I guess that about wraps it up," said the voice in the darknesss. "The bank is expecting the cavalrymen day after tomorrow. You boys ought to light out of here early in the morning. Be near Tucson tomorrow night, ready to intercept the army at the pass."

"How about the haircuts, boss?" asked Becker.

"I'll get Hube Farley outta bed at sunup," butted in Evans. "He can shave you boys and cut your hair at the shop. We can still leave early enough to camp on the north side of Tucson tomorrow night."

"I have one other idea," said Dave Sundeen, looking toward the shadowed figure.

"Shoot."

"Let's take about a dozen hats with us to the pass."

"Hats?" echoed the boss.

"We can place them among the rocks above the road. Make it look like we've got an army."

"Hey, that's a great idea!" exclaimed the boss, almost forgetting to whisper. "Mack, you take Neal and go bust into Thurston's place. Get a dozen hats."

Furman began to stir.

"See you when you get back with the half-million, Sundeen," said the boss.

"But will I see *you*?" asked Sundeen caustically.

The man in the shadows snickered but did not answer.

The sun had colored the eastern horizon a rich yellow when Mack Evans and the three freshly barbered men rode north out of Tombstone toward Tucson.

Dave Sundeen had rousted Deputy Ralph Stine before sunup, advising Stine that he would be out of town on business for a couple of days. Sundeen did not want to attract suspicion of any kind by just riding away. He thought it best to stay on as acting sheriff for a short time after the robbery, then resign and leave Tombstone.

He would suggest to Mack Evans that they ride north when the gang rode away from the bound and gagged hostages. When they passed out of sight, they could double back south. They would take the victims' horses along with them. It would take them some time to untie themselves and walk to Tucson. Dave figured this would give him ample time to play out the acting-sheriff part long enough so that he could ride from Tombstone without arousing suspicion. Sundeen was to meet Evans and the others about five miles north of Tombstone.

Some two miles northeast of the point where the

outlaws rode out of town, a lone rider squinted at their distant forms.

Tombstone was beginning to bustle as the rider moved slowly onto Allen Street. Like a well-oiled machine, he slipped from the saddle and entered two saloons before he reached the Capitol.

When the batwings emitted their familiar squeak, Bert Riley looked toward the door.

Standing tall and raw-boned was the unmistakable figure of a gunslinger. But this one was a bit different from the usual. His guns were holstered *butts-forward* on his lean thighs. His steel-gray eyes were deeply socketed above prominent cheekbones. His lips were thin and colorless, drawn tight beneath a dark pencil-line moustache.

Riley ran his palm over his bald scalp. There were no customers in the saloon.

Approaching the bartender, the slender gunman spoke with a voice as emotionless as his face: "I'm looking for a dude named Dan Colt."

CHAPTER FIFTEEN

"Dan Colt?" Riley echoed nervously. "There used to be a gunslinger by that name."

"That's the dude," said Ric Baron coldly.

"If he'd been in Tombstone, I'd know it, sir," said Riley, "but there's been no word about it."

"He came here all right. I got it on good authority."

"Maybe he's on his way. Not here yet."

"He was riding ahead of me. I'm here, ain't I?" Baron's manner was threatening.

"Why don't you check some of the other saloons? Maybe he's been—"

"I already checked with two," interrupted the gunslinger, his face rigid. "They gave me the same thing."

"Sorry, mister. I just can't help you. Why don't you talk to the sheriff? He always knows when a famous gunman is in town."

"Does he know I'm here?" Baron asked, widening his eyes.

"Well, I can't say, sir. I haven't seen him today . . . and besides, I don't—"

"You don't know who I am?"

"Well, no. I—"

"Baron! Ric Baron, barman. The name familiar to you?"

"I've heard of *Vic* Baron, but—"

"He was my brother," said Ric, baring his teeth.

"W–was?"

"This Colt dude shot him in the back up in Utah," Ric lied. "Snuck up on him and put a bullet between his shoulder blades."

"I–I'm sorry," stammered the bartender. "That's a mighty low thing to do."

"Where's this sheriff's office?" Baron asked, turning toward the doorway.

"Down the street, on the left," answered Riley, pointing. "You can't miss it. Regular sheriff is on leave of absence. Got shot a few days ago."

"That's too bad," said Ric facetiously.

"Acting sheriff and deputies are there," said Riley, his voice trailing off as Ric Baron disappeared through the door.

Ralph Stine was sitting at the desk, cleaning a Remington .44, as Ric Baron stepped through the open door of the office.

"Sheriff in?" Baron asked with a saucy tone, his face taut.

"He's home, recuperating from a gunshot," Stine answered in a friendly manner.

"I mean the *acting* sheriff," snapped Baron.

The deputy studied him for a moment. "You fall out of the wrong side of the bed, pardner?"

Baron's jaw squared and his eyes widened. "Don't smartmouth me, Deputy. I ain't your partner. I asked you a question."

"It's not your question that bothers me, mister. It's the tone of your voice. Now I don't know who stuck the burr in your long johns, but it wasn't me." Stine stood up. "Acting sheriff is out of town. If you'll friendly-up a little bit, I'll see if I can help you."

Ric Baron opened his mouth to speak when the sound of Slim Pardee's boots on the boardwalk made him check his tongue. The deputy slipped past Baron.

"Mornin', Ralph," said Pardee, casting an impervious glance at the tall, slender gunslinger. "Dave in yet?"

"He's outta town," replied Stine, looking at his fellow deputy, then back to Baron.

Slim walked to the potbellied stove and picked up the cold coffeepot. "Thought you'd have the coffee hot, Ralph," he said with light annoyance.

"I'm looking for a tall blond hombre," interrupted Baron. "Name's Colt. Dan Colt."

"You're lookin' in the wrong place," said Stine. "Dan Colt was killed by bushwackers several years ago, back Kansas way. Or is there some other fella by that name?"

"Rumor about that ambush was wrong," said Baron evenly. "He's alive. He came to Tombstone just recently."

Stine rubbed his freshly shaven chin. "You say he's tall and blond?"

Ric nodded. "Built like a steam engine. Has pale blue eyes that look right through you. Wears a pair of twin Colts."

Slim Pardee set the cold coffeepot back on the equally cold stove. "Sounds like you're describing our acting sheriff, mister," he said, hitching up his pants.

"Told us his name's Dave Sundeen," said Stine.

Baron nodded. "That's his alias," he said, pulling a long, thin cigar from his shirt pocket. "He was using the name over in Utah, where he shot my brother."

"Oh?" said Stine.

"Yeah . . . *in the back*," said Baron, grinding his teeth.

"You aiming to challenge him?" asked Pardee.

The thought sent a chill down Baron's spine. He fished in his vest pocket for a match, thumbnailed it into flame, and lit the cigar. Giving a wrong answer here could rebound in disaster later if things went wrong.

Baron puffed heavily, filling the room with blue smoke. "Just want to see him," he said, casting Slim a withering glance.

"He'll be back in a day or two," said Stine advisedly.

"Thanks," said Baron, turning toward the door. "I'll wait around." He dissolved through the door in a cloud of smoke.

It was nearly nine o'clock when Neal Furman, perched on a high rock, caught the first sign of the cavalry detail. Squinting against the morning sunlight, he waited until he was certain. Soon the small cloud of dust in the background revealed six dark figures, one leading and five following.

Furman looked into the shaded narrow passageway below. Mack Evans stood with head thrust forward, talking to Dave Sundeen. Otis Becker was descending a crude path between the rocks, where he had strategically placed six hats, weighing down the brims with stones. Dick Millard was just finishing an identical task on the opposite side.

"Mack!" shouted Furman, cupping his hands around his mouth. "They're comin'!"

Evans tilted his big shaggy head back, looked up at Furman, and shouted, "How many?"

"Six!" came the reply.

The huge man waved for Furman to descend and spoke to Sundeen. "The boss's information is seldom wrong. We'd better get ready."

"Hats are in place, Mack," said Becker, approaching.

"Good," replied Evans, casting a glance up the steep, rocky grade. Studying both sides for a moment, he chuckled. "Gotta hand it to you, Dave. I'd swear there was a dozen sharpshooters up there among them rocks, just waitin' to pull triggers."

Sundeen smiled. "Let's hope those troopers think so."

The horses had been picketed at the south end of the pass, far enough away so that there would be no danger of their catching the scent of the cavalry horses and spoiling the surprise.

Becker and Millard were stationed on the east side, just below the scattered hats. Furman was in a corresponding position on the west side. Mack Evans and Dave Sundeen were concealed behind boulders at the north entrance of Half-Moon Pass.

Soon the sound of shod hooves on rocks rang in the air, accompanied by squeaking leather. Within moments the blue-clad troopers rounded the rock curvature, heading into the pass.

Instantly Evans and Sundeen leaped onto the road, guns drawn. The lieutenant jerked his mount to a halt, the others following suit.

"We want you to climb off those horses real gentle-like," bellowed the burly Evans.

The officer eyed them furiously. "What's this all about?" he demanded, face flushing. The blaze-faced bay he rode danced nervously.

"I said peel off them horses!" Evans roared fiercely.

One of the troopers palmed the stock of his carbine, pulling it from the scabbard.

"I wouldn't do that, Corporal!" shouted Dave Sundeen. "Better take a look up in those rocks," he said with a toss of his head.

The corporal curbed his move, the muzzle still in the scabbard. All six mounted men lifted their gaze upward. The lieutenant's face blanched. Tugging at the brim of his campaign hat with the crossed-sabers insignia, he spoke with deliberate agitation. "I don't know what you're after, but I remind you, you're molesting the United States Army. I'll see you hanged for this!"

"If all them itchy-fingered hombres in them rocks start shootin', lieutenant, you won't see nuthin'!" bellowed Evans. "Now you jist climb down nice and easy."

Turning in the saddle, the lieutenant spoke with trepidation. "All right, men. Dismount."

While Mack Evans held the officer at gunpoint, Sundeen approached the five enlisted men, motioning them away from their horses. "Lift the pistols from your holsters and drop 'em," Dave commanded. As the troopers complied, he said, "Now walk up toward those rocks."

When all five were in the deep shade of the rock wall, Sundeen studied them for a moment. Pulling the smallest man from the rest, he said to the others, "Now you four take off your uniforms!"

"Now you look here!" one of them blurted. "You ain't got no business—"

Sundeen took a step forward and clouted the man across the mouth with his right-hand revolver. "Peel 'em off!" he said indignantly.

As the four troopers disrobed, Evans lifted the lieutenant's revolver, broke the action, and punched out the cartridges. Pocketing them, he snapped the gun and placed it back in the holster. He also emptied the officer's reserve pouch and dropped those cartridges into the same pocket.

"Am I to disrobe too?" the lieutenant asked Evans icily.

"Nope," retorted the huge man. "You're gonna do what you started out to do."

Suddenly the picture came into focus. The officer's

features stiffened. "It'll never work," he said, glaring hard at Evans's bearded face.

"If it doesn't, you'll bury five dead troopers," said the big man.

Evans glanced at the quartet now standing in their long underwear. Lifting his voice, he said, "All right, boys! Come down and change clothes!"

As Sundeen, Furman, Millard, and Becker fitted themselves into uniforms, hats, and boots, Mack Evans spoke loudly enough for all to hear.

"Lieutenant, I'm going to say this only once . . . by the way, what's yore handle?"

"Eastwood," replied the officer heavily. "Duane Eastwood."

"Okay, Eastwood. Hear me good," said Evans. "These four will ride as your men. You will fill them in on what to do while you ride to Tucson. You will bring the Fargo men and the money right back here."

Eastwood cast a helpless glance toward his perplexed troopers.

"If you mess it up," continued Evans harshly, "I'll be here with 'em. So help me, *I'll kill 'em all.*" Looking the young officer straight in the eye, he said, "You understand?"

"They'll ask questions," said Eastwood.

"Whaddya mean?" the bulky man asked, his face clouding.

"They asked for *six* men. This makes only *five*," said the lieutenant solemnly. "Why don't you send another man along?"

A broad, wicked smile spread over Evans's big face. "'Cause we ain't got another man."

"What about all those—" The truth sprang like a trap in Eastwood's mind, registering instantly on his face. He shot a hard glare upward at the lifeless hats among the rocks and cursed.

Mack Evans burst into a heavy belly-laugh. The other outlaws joined in as the six troopers looked on in an admixture of fear and disgust.

Regaining his composure, the huge man eyed Eastwood and said, "You tell 'em you left the fort with six, but one man was sick and had to turn back. Got it?"

"But what if they—?"

"You'd better convince 'em." Evans's eyes were hard.

After tying up the troopers and hiding the extra horse, the four outlaws mounted the cavalry horses and headed for Tucson. Dave Sundeen rode directly behind Lieutenant Eastwood. Otis Becker complained that his boots were too tight.

The sun was almost overhead when Lieutenant Duane Eastwood rode up to the First National Bank of Tucson.

"I am supposed to report to the bank's president," said Eastwood. "He will send someone to bring the Fargo men. They're staying at one of the hotels."

Neal Furman started to dismount.

"Hold it, you idiot!" snapped Eastwood in a half-whisper. "Everybody dismounts in unison when I give the command."

Furman checked himself and cursed. Sundeen shot him a stern look. The street was busy with people.

"I have to go in alone," advised Eastwood cautiously.

Sundeen started to protest. The lieutenant continued hastily. "It's normal procedure. You men will wait here and look alert."

"You peep a word in there, soldier boy, and you've bought graves for your men," Sundeen said, scowling.

"You needn't worry, *Corporal*," Eastwood sneered. "I know when the cards are stacked against me." Taking a deep breath, he said loudly, "Companeeee . . . dismount!"

Curious eyes watched from both sides of the dusty street as the "troopers" clustered in front of the bank.

Lieutenant Eastwood disappeared through the door.

CHAPTER SIXTEEN

Otis Becker was complaining to the other outlaws about the tight army boots when a young man emerged from the bank. He cast an approving eye at the four uniformed men and darted up the street.

Duane Eastwood, whose hair and complexion somewhat resembled that of Dave Sundeen, stepped into the bright Arizona sunlight.

"Fargo men will be here in a few minutes," Eastwood said on approach. "President isn't too happy about us being minus one trooper. Said the Fargo representatives may object and demand coverage as promised by my commanding officer."

Sundeen ran his hand over his heavy blond moustache. "Like the big ugly man said, you *better* convince 'em," Dave warned.

Presently the runner appeared on the street, accelerating toward the bank. Pausing to acknowledge the lieutenant, he said hurriedly, "They are going to the livery for their horses now, sir. They will be along in a few moments."

"Thank you," replied Eastwood, wondering if the boy had heard him as the door quickly closed. The young lieutenant paced the boardwalk nervously, touching the brim of his hat as two young ladies passed by.

Dave Sundeen was thinking how awkward he felt without his twin Colts. A single gun worn high on his waist felt like a strange growth on his side. He would be glad to get this thing over with and get back into civilian attire.

Strangely enough, at this same moment Sundeen found himself thinking of Molly Jo Wyler. He could see her freshly scrubbed face in his mind's eye, shining sweetly in the Utah sun. An ineffable feeling crept over him. Had she really meant something to him? *Couldn't have,* he told himself. *She's too young. Besides—* His thoughts were interrupted when Dick Millard broke the silence.

"Here they come," said Millard, pointing to two well-dressed men approaching on horseback. "Must be them. They look the type."

As the two men reined in next to the army horses, Eastwood said, "Let me do the talking."

"Gentlemen," said the older of the two. He was a medium-sized man in his late fifties. His hair was snowy white, which contrasted sharply with his bushy black eyebrows.

Lieutenant Eastwood stepped toward them, offering his hand to the man as he dismounted. "I am Lieutenant Duane Eastwood," he said, smiling.

"I am Harry Forbes of Wells Fargo," said the white-haired man. "And this is Charles Stone."

Stone, who looked to be in his early forties, extended a bony hand, offering a weak smile.

Eastwood, turning and pointing to Sundeen, Furman, Becker, and Millard respectively, said, "Mr. Forbes . . . Mr. Stone . . . this is trooper Hollingsworth, trooper Brickman, trooper Ames, and trooper Knudsen."

The four outlaws regarded the Fargo men soberly, dipping their chins.

Instantly Harry Forbes cast a disapproving eye at the group. "We asked for six men, Lieutenant. Is there another?"

"Well, sir," said Eastwood with military poise, "we left the fort with six, but one man became ill after several hours and had to return. It would have meant at least a one-day delay to go back for another man. I decided that since I had four of the most experienced men with me, we would come ahead."

Forbes rubbed his chin. Looking to his partner, he said, "What do you think, Charlie?"

"It's up to you, sir," said Stone. "We sure need to have the money there on time."

Forbes turned abruptly and said, "All right, Lieutenant. Let's get the money and be on our way."

Ten minutes later the Wells Fargo men emerged from the First National Bank, each carrying a pair of saddle bags. The lieutenant followed them.

Otis Becker said in a whisper, "Them bags ain't big enough to hold half a million in payroll denominations!"

"We'll find out right quick," whispered Furman.

"Right now we're supposed to pull and cock these rifles," said Sundeen.

Four army carbines were unsheathed and cocked in unison.

As the saddle bags were being strapped into place on the Fargo horses, Neal Furman said, "I beg your pardon, Mr. Forbes, but ain't we supposed to be haulin' half a million dollars?"

"Keep your voice down, trooper!" Forbes said, glowering. "We *are* carrying that amount."

"Must be in big bills," said Becker in a hushed tone.

Looking around to see if they had any observers, Forbes replied, "This is a payroll, gentlemen. Mostly fifties and twenties."

"But how—?"

Becker was interrupted by Charles Stone. "It's all in brand-new bills, Ames. They pack tighter when they've never been used."

Becker's eye caught Sundeen's. Brand-new currency would have successive serial numbers. They could easily be spotted and tracked. The boss would be unhappy to learn this. It would mean no spending in the Arizona Territory until a good deal of time had passed.

Dave scanned the faces of the others. They, too, registered comprehension. Sundeen shrugged his shoulders slightly, tilting his head.

Eastwood swung into his saddle and barked, "Ames . . . Knudsen . . . Brickman . . . you ride behind these men. Hollingsworth and I will ride in front."

Bridles tinkled and leather squeaked as the seven men rode out of Tucson, the warm midday sun on their backs.

Nearly an hour had passed when the trail began to climb and wind through steep hills and tall rock formations. The horses smelled water and nickered.

"Might as well let them get a good drink," said Eastwood, pointing to a gurgling shallow stream ahead.

"I could use one myself," said Dick Millard. "The water in this canteen is bitter."

The seven men dismounted where the stream rounded a sharp bend. Letting the horses drink, they took their own fill.

Dave Sundeen stood up, having knelt to drink, and wiped water from his mouth. His eye caught movement on a rock formation about thirty feet above the stream. Just as he focused in on the man, he saw the muzzle of the rifle.

"Every one of you drop them guns and reach for the sky!" the rifleman bawled.

Harry Forbes turned up a stricken face, which went pallid instantly.

Sundeen saw two more men descending upon them. They were coming around giant boulders just below the man with the rifle. Each one of the outlaws posing as troopers had his carbine in hand.

Harry Forbes, in blind panic, bolted to his horse and swung into the saddle. A rifle barked above. Forbes had his horse in the stream. The Wells Fargo man straightened momentarily in the saddle, then rolled off sideways, landing facedown in six-inch-deep water.

In the meantime Dave Sundeen swiveled the carbine muzzle upward and fired. The other two men did an instant about-face and dove behind some boulders. Up on the rock the man dropped his rifle, stood erect, teetered for a moment, and plunged over. His body hit the stream with a flat, popping sound.

The lieutenant hastily lifted the rifle from its boot on Forbes's horse.

Millard, Becker, and Furman were returning shots toward the boulders as the two above opened fire. Duane Eastwood was dragging Charles Stone toward the bend in the stream, attempting to get him out of the line of fire.

A fourth ambusher appeared out of nowhere on the tall rock where the first one had appeared. Dropping to one knee, he began shooting at Eastwood and Stone. The lieutenant took a bullet in the right shoulder. The force of the impact knocked him down. He rolled over in the water and returned a shot. Rock shattered near the toe of the ambusher's boot. The man's gun roared again and Stone let out a death cry.

Sundeen's rifle belched fire. A dark hole appeared suddenly in the man's forehead. The rifle clattered on the stony surface and slid over the edge, falling into the stream. The ambusher fell face forward, his body sprawling on a rock formation. His head dangled over the edge, spewing blood.

Dave's attention was drawn to Millard, Becker, and Furman, who were pinned down under rapid fire. The horses had now scattered. Dave thought of the saddle bags bearing five hundred thousand dollars. For the moment the money had to be secondary. The two ambushers nestled in the boulders demanded attention.

The tall man made a hasty dive toward the base of a giant rock. Once under its protection he shot a glance at Duane Eastwood, who was sitting in the middle of the stream, holding his shoulder. Blood was oozing between his fingers. Forbes's rifle lay on the bottom of the stream.

Sundeen's three cohorts had the full attention of the ambushers for the moment. He waded to Eastwood, gently picked him up, and half-carried him to the base of the rock formation. Easing him into the stream, Dave said, "Nowhere else to put you for the moment. You'll be wet, but they can't see you here."

Sundeen eyed the wounded shoulder. "Pretty bad?"

"Can't tell," answered the lieutenant, grimacing.

Gunfire continued as Dave waded downstream along the sheer rock wall. After covering about fifty yards, he found a break in the wall. Slowly he climbed upward, slipping from time to time. After several moments he reached the top and hastened toward the roaring guns.

Within seconds he found a spot directly above the two ambushers. Bellying down on the warm stone surface, he pointed his carbine at their backs and shouted, "That's enough! Drop 'em!"

Both men turned and looked up, shock registering on their faces. The one to Sundeen's right quickly brought his rifle to bear. The tall man's gun spit instant death. As the man fell in a crumpled heap, his partner threw down his own rifle. Hoisting his hands above his head, he cried, "Don't shoot! Don't shoot!"

Looking toward the three prostrate outlaws dressed as troopers, Sundeen hollered, "It's all right, boys! I got 'em!"

Dick Millard stood up, blood showing on the sleeve of his left forearm. Otis Becker hoisted his thick frame upward. His gaze was on Neal Furman, who lay motionless on the ground. Furman's hat was askew. Dave knew he was dead.

"All right, mister," Sundeen said to the ambusher, "walk down there slow-like."

Hands over head, the man began to descend the craggy pathway toward Millard and Becker.

"Here he comes, fellas," Sundeen called loudly. "The other one's dead!"

As Millard tended to his bleeding arm, Becker pointed his rifle at the approaching ambusher. When the man reached ground level, Sundeen hollered, "You watch him, Otis. I'm coming down."

Just as Dave knelt down to begin his descent, he heard Becker's gun roar. Springing to his feet, he saw the ambusher lying face up, his sightless eyes staring at the brassy sky.

Becker focused on Sundeen. As blue smoke lifted from the rifle's muzzle, the hulky man said with tight lips, "He killed Neal."

Wordlessly Dave descended to the stream.

The bodies of Forbes, Stone, and the first ambusher bobbed limply in the shallow water. Duane Eastwood remained where Sundeen had left him.

"How's the arm, Dick?" Dave asked Millard.

"Just a scratch. It'll be all right," Millard answered.

Otis Becker looked southward across the stream. All seven horses had clustered near a patch of greasewood about a hundred yards away. The hulky man sighed with relief. Turning toward Dave Sundeen, who now had Eastwood on his feet, Becker said, "Horses are all down there."

"Yeah, I saw 'em," said Sundeen.

Carefully lowering the lieutenant to a reclining position, Dave tore the shirt open, exposing the wound. Eastwood ground his teeth as the tall man explored the area.

"Bullet went clean through, Lieutenant. You'll be all right if we get you to a doctor right away."

Eastwood's jaw slackened. Eyes wide, he said, "You're going to take me to a doctor?"

"Yep. I can have you back in Tucson in a jiffy."

"What kind of outlaw are you?" asked Eastwood through clenched teeth.

"That's what I want to know!" snapped Otis Becker.

Sundeen turned slowly, setting his blue gaze on Becker's face. The bulky man's eyes flashed fire.

"We ain't got time to pamper no kid soldier, Dave. I say leave him be. If he can walk to town, let him. If not, tough stuff." Nodding northward, he said, "Let's get the horses and light a shuck outta here."

"He'd never make it," observed Sundeen with a hard stare.

"Then let him die," slashed Dick Millard.

Dave Sundeen stood to full height. Anger was lifting inside him. "I may be an outlaw, but I'm not a murderer. This man will bleed to death if he doesn't get medical attention. If we leave him, we're guilty of murder."

Becker's hard-featured face twisted. "But—"

"*I'll* take him, Becker," Sundeen said curtly. "You two take Neal's body and the money. Leave my clothes and guns with my horse. I'll tell the doctor in Tucson about these other bodies. He can pass the word to the sheriff. After I see that the lieutenant here is properly cared for, I'll be on my way."

Becker shook his head. "Okay, Dave. Have it your way."

Within a quarter hour the horses were gathered.

Sundeen sat behind Eastwood, supporting him. A second horse followed on a lead rope. Reining southward, Sundeen looked back at Becker and Millard, who were preparing to mount up. "Tell Mack I'll meet you at the hideout tomorrow night after dark."

Becker nodded.

"Tell him to have my share of the money ready," said Dave, fixing an icy stare on the thick-bodied man.

Becker fought an evil smile, which won out and curled his thick lips. Dave's eyes flashed to Millard. The slender face showed nothing.

As Sundeen looked back at Otis Becker, the ugly man said, "I'll tell him."

Slowly Dave Sundeen and the wounded lieutenant rode away, leaving the two outlaws in animated conversation.

CHAPTER SEVENTEEN

The stars were beginning to twinkle brightly as Dave Sundeen left the road, angling in the direction of the old ranch house that served as a hideout. The last glimmer of light had died on the western horizon. Presently the moon sent its preamble of yellow haze on the opposite horizon. Within minutes the moon itself appeared as a golden rim. By the time the hideout was in sight, the yellow disc in the night sky had released its touch on the earth, glided upward, and turned silver.

Sundeen reined the buckskin about two hundred yards from the thicket of mesquite which surrounded the ranch house. A light shimmered through the trees from one of the windows.

All day long the wicked smile that Dave had seen on Otis Becker's face had picked at his mind, like a buzzard tearing raw meat. Had he been set up for a double-cross? Why the boss's dogged resistance to Dave's knowing his identity?

Somewhere in the back of his consciousness, a tiny danger signal was making itself heard. The setup was coming into focus. Dave Sundeen would go along on the robbery as gunblazing insurance on the promise of a hundred thousand dollars. After the money was safe in hand, he would be dealt death instead. If he had been considered as part of the gang, he would have been included in the boss's confidence.

In case of a slip-up in the master plan, Dave might evade their death trap. The boss had roots in Tombstone. The others didn't. If Sundeen lived to take vengeance, the gang would easily scatter. The boss could carry on his business in Tombstone, undetected and unidentified.

Dave looked at the moon as a coyote yelped in the distance. He shook his head. Maybe this was all in his imagination. Maybe this kind of thinking was awry.

The little signal screamed again.

Dismounting where he had halted the buckskin, Dave ground-reined the gelding and proceeded cautiously on foot. Reflexively he lifted the twin Colts and eased them back in their holsters.

Quietly picking his way through the mesquite trees, he approached the house from the back side. The bedroom windows were dark. The only window exuding light was that at the end of the hallway, which led from the main room to the bedrooms. This was the same hallway where the boss had veiled himself three nights earlier.

As Dave approached the window, he saw that it was open about eight inches. Voices inside rose briefly, then fell to a low murmur.

The man with the twin Colts could see one end of the table. Dick Millard was sitting at that end, his left arm bandaged and resting in a crude sling. A part of one man's shoulder was in view; Dave thought it was Otis Becker's.

Putting his ear to the open window, Sundeen heard Mack Evans's deep voice.

"Either way, boss," said Evans, "it'll have to be in the back."

"That's for sure," Becker's throaty voice chimed in. "Ain't none of us gonna face him head on."

Sundeen's heart leaped to his throat. The boss was in there!

You were right, Sundeen, he thought to himself. *They're planning to do you in!*

Dave strained his ears, waiting for the boss to speak.

"After the way he took out them four hardcases that day he rode into Tombstone, there's no way I'd want to stand up to him," put in Dick Millard.

"If he comes here tonight, boss," said Mack Evans, "why don't you take the shotgun and sit in the dark like you did the other night? We'll maneuver him into position and you blow him to kingdom come."

The boss spoke, but Dave could not make out what he said. The voice was too subdued to recognize.

Again the conversation dropped to a murmur. One of the men coughed. Another cleared his throat. Dick Millard lifted a whiskey bottle and took a deep gulp. Mack Evans laughed.

Dave shifted his position. The voices rose and lowered in volume repeatedly. Sundeen was able to piece together that the boss had stashed the five hundred thousand under the floorboards of an old abandoned house in town.

The man listening at the window remembered that Tombstone had a good number of abandoned houses.

A coyote howled at the moon somewhere out on the desert.

Suddenly the boss spoke up clearly and said, "We can't leave the money there, but until I find a better place, the old house will do."

Dave Sundeen's head jerked. With his mouth hanging open, he shook his head. *It can't be!* he said to himself.

Mack Evans said, "I sure hate to think of havin' to wait over a year to spend that money."

Becker said something Dave could not distinguish.

"Got any ideas where you'll stash it for all that time, boss?" asked Millard.

"Not yet," said the familiar voice. "But I'll think of a place. A good safe place."

Sundeen was still trying to believe his ears when a chair scraped on the floor and a pair of wide shoulders appeared. The man walked to the back door of the house, opened it, and looked out into the darkness. His face was fully illuminated by the lantern light. After several moments he turned around and closed the door.

Dave had taken a good look and now shook his head again.

Standing in the same spot, the boss said, "If he doesn't show up tonight, we'll set up a time to turn over his share and kill him when he comes to collect."

The other voices spoke in agreement as Sundeen wheeled and headed through the trees in the direction of his horse.

Swinging into the saddle, he fostered a plan to corner the boss alone and needle the location of the money out of him. The simple threat to expose him to the town would probably be enough. If not, there were other ways. Sundeen had run with outlaws long enough to learn how to loosen a man's tongue.

Dave Sundeen arose from his bed in the Arizona Hotel shortly before sunup. While he shaved, the plan finalized in his mind. He would surprise the boss of the gang by bursting in on him before the double-dealing scoundrel was out of bed. As acting sheriff Dave had learned the homes of all the prominent citizens of Tombstone.

The sun was lifting its orange rim over the horizon as the tall man left the hotel and walked to the livery. Aware that he might have to leave town in a hurry, he would ride the buckskin to the boss's house.

In the saddle Dave rode past the Arizona Hotel.

James Louis Rountree had just reported for work. He waved to Dave through the lobby window. Sundeen returned the gesture.

No one was moving about on the streets as yet. That is, to the knowledge of Dave Sundeen.

The twin brother of Dan Colt was not aware that he had been observed entering the hotel late the night before. At this moment a pair of dark, vitriolic eyes peered at him from the corner of the Arizona . . . eyes that took him for Dan Colt.

Ric Baron waited until the tall man on the buckskin rode past the hotel. Lining the sights of the rifle on his broad back, he squeezed the trigger. The sound of the shot echoed and reverberated among false-fronted buildings.

Baron, undetected, ran down the alley to the Great Western Hotel, where he had rented a room. Hastening up the outside stairway, he slipped through the hallway door. No one was in sight. Wiping sweat from his forehead, he dashed into his room.

The cowardly Baron waited in the room until his breathing had returned to normal. Splashing cold water from the basin into his face, he dried it with a towel. As he ran a comb through his hair, he observed his face in the mirror. A truculent smile parted his colorless lips.

"I took care of it for you, brother Vic," he said, laughing viciously. "He paid for killing you. Now Dan Colt is dead!"

Donning his black flat-crowned hat, Ric Baron left the room and casually descended the stairs to the lobby. The clerk and four other people were standing outside on the boardwalk, talking excitedly and looking up the street.

"What happened?" asked the lean-bodied gunslinger, feigning ignorance.

"Somebody shot Sheriff Sundeen," answered one of the observers.

"Kill him?" queried Baron with a casual tone.

"Think so," said the same person.

Ric clicked his tongue. "Too bad." Slowly Baron made his way toward the crowd.

The buckskin gelding's eyes were dilated. The hostler had come to take the horse to the stable. The animal clearly was aware that something bad had happened to its master and was refusing to leave the scene.

Moving in close, Baron could see a man he supposed to be the doctor bending over the fallen man. Standing nearest to Dave Sundeen's bloody prostrate form were Bennett Crabtree, John Springer, and Elrod Frame.

The doctor spoke to Sheriff John Springer. "John, have your deputies carry him to my office."

Ralph Stine and Slim Pardee stepped in without a word from Springer. Carefully they hoisted Dave Sundeen and, followed by the doctor and James Louis Rountree, headed for the doctor's office.

With tears streaming down his dark cheeks, Rountree hobbled alongside the doctor, saying, "Ah had jis waved to him out da window, doctah. Den *bam!* Some dihty low-down snake done shot him!"

Ric Baron eyed the star on Springer's vest. "Sheriff, is the man still alive?" he asked calmly. Inside he was churning wildly.

"Just barely," came the answer.

Springer followed the group to the doctor's office. Ric Baron watched them vanish through the door. The crowd dispersed, showing little concern over the incident.

For three hours Baron sat across the street on a bench and smoked his long, slim cigars. No one seemed to notice his vigil. Presently Sheriff Springer and the two deputies stepped through the door and angled across the street toward the sheriff's office.

Ric sprang to his feet when the black man emerged and headed for the hotel. Baron intercepted Rountree at the boardwalk in front of the Arizona.

"How is the man?" the gunslinger asked apprehensively.

Rountree looked at him with swollen eyes. "He's dead, mistah," he said, wagging his head. "He's dead."

The next morning at ten o'clock, the watchful killer loitered in the street until he saw the somber black hearse pull out from behind the funeral parlor and proceed slowly north up Fremont Street. Through the glass he caught a glimpse of an unpainted pine box.

James Louis Rountree rode on the seat of the hearse with the undertaker. Only three riders made up the procession: Sheriff John Springer and his two deputies.

People along the way gave the hearse a casual glance. No one outside of the funeral party seemed to care.

Ric Baron returned to his hotel room and stretched out on the bed. He was pleased with himself. "Dan Colt, alias Dave Sundeen, is deader than a doornail," he said aloud.

Late in the afternoon, after a couple drinks at the Capitol, Baron nonchalantly rode his horse north on Fremont.

The sun projected long, slanted shadows over Boot Hill. A stiff breeze skipped little swirls of dust across the road as Ric Baron turned his horse into the gloomy graveyard. Instantly his eye caught the fresh mound of dirt. Sliding from the saddle in his usual cool manner, the cowardly Baron threaded his way through the dismal gravemarkers.

A dissolute smile was etched on his face as Vic Baron's vengeful brother stood over the grave and read the crude marker:

> HERE LIES
> DAVE SUNDEEN,
> SHOT BY SOMEBODY
> HE NEVER SEEN.

"Wherever you are, Vic, I know you feel better now," the kid said audibly. "And to make you feel even better, I'm gonna stay here for the next three days." His eyes were wild, almost insane. "And I'm gonna come out here three times a day and spit on his grave!"

The immature Baron knew no other way to vent his seething, volcanic hatred for the man who killed the brother he worshiped.

Rolling his tongue in his mouth, the long, lean youth wearing Colt revolvers butts-forward spit several times on the fresh mound.

The next day Ric Baron rode to Boot Hill just after breakfast, at high noon, and again at sundown. Each time, with a crazy, wild look in his dark eyes, he spit repeatedly on the grave of Dave Sundeen.

CHAPTER EIGHTEEN

On the second day of Ric Baron's rampage of demented expectorations, Dan Colt rode into Tombstone in the middle of the afternoon.

Ric Baron was napping lazily in his room at the Great Western.

The afternoon was hot and few people were about. Dan rode down Fremont Street unnoticed. His hopes of finding his outlaw twin in this rugged frontier town were running high. Dave had come to Tombstone for a particular term of employment. Dan had no idea whether it was good or bad, but if it detained him long enough for Dan to catch him, the result would be good.

Eyeing the saloons as he guided the big black gelding along the street, Dan saw quickly that the Capitol was the most popular place. He would start there.

Elbowing his way through the batwings, he paused inside the door, allowing his eyes to adjust to the dim light. The place was nearly full. No music was being played at the moment, but the usual din of idle chatter, interrupted by an occasional burst of laughter, met Colt's ears.

Suddenly someone said something the tall man could not discern. Within five seconds every eye was fastened on him and the silence was obvious.

In the long months of trailing his twin, Dan had become accustomed to people thinking he was Dave.

There was no doubt in his mind: His brother had been here.

As he stepped toward the bar, seven men backed away, slackjawed, eyes bulging.

What in the world did he do here? Dan asked himself.

Bert Riley took hold of the bar to steady himself. Sweat beaded on his bald head.

Reading the cold terror in the bartender's eyes, Dan said, "You know where there's a man looks like me?"

Riley worked his jaw but could not find his voice.

No one moved from the tables. Each man sat as if he were frozen. Dan set his pale blue gaze on the cluster of men standing at the bar.

"Any of you ever see a man looks like me?" The seven were breathless.

The batwings squeaked behind the tall man. Dan turned to face the newcomer. It was Elrod Frame.

Immediately Frame's eyes fell on Dan Colt's leathery features. He checked his stride, mouth agape. His face took on a similar color to his hoary head. Dan started to speak to him, when Frame suddenly gained control of his senses, wheeled, and shot through the door. Every man in the saloon could hear him running down the street shouting, "Sheriff! Sheriff! Sheriff!"

Dan turned, swept the room with an icy glare, and shouldered his way through the batwings. He decided the sheriff would be his best bet. He hoped the man would not try to arrest him for something that Dave had done.

As Dan stepped into the street, he saw the frightened man dash through the door under a sign that read, SHERIFF'S OFFICE AND JAIL.

Releasing the reins from the hitchrail, Dan led his horse down the street toward John Springer's office.

People responding to the excitement were looking through dusty windows. Others stepped out onto the board sidewalk.

Dan heard a feminine gasp. Three doors slammed almost simultaneously.

Presently two young men emerged from the sheriff's office, wearing deputy's badges. The breathless silver-haired man was peering over their shoulders from the doorway. Both lawmen looked stunned.

"Have you two got enough manhood in you to tell me what's going on here?" asked Colt.

Ralph Stine spoke from the side of his mouth, eyes fixed on the tall, blue-eyed man. "Mr. Frame, you go on back to your office."

Elrod Frame rubbed the exterior wall of the sheriff's office with his back. Stumbling clumsily, he left the scene.

With his eyes still lined on Dan's face, Stine spoke to his partner. "Go get the sheriff."

Slim Pardee edged his way up the street. "I never believed in this kind of thing before," he said tremulously, "but this . . ." He swallowed hard and broke into a run.

"What's he talking about?" Dan asked, wrapping the gelding's reins around the hitchrail.

"You're not Dave Sundeen," said Stine, wagging his head. It was not a question; it was a statement designed to bolster his own courage.

"Common mistake," said Dan with a sigh. "I'm his brother."

"B–b–brother?"

"Yeah. *Twin* brother, as you can see."

Stine's face muscles relaxed. He took a deep breath and exhaled it slowly through pursed lips. "I think you'd better come inside."

Dan followed the deputy through the door.

"Sit down," said Stine, pointing at a straight-backed chair. Dan sat down in the chair and pushed his hat off his brow.

"Want some coffee?" asked the deputy. "It's not steaming, but it's still on the warm side."

"Sure," replied the blond man. " 'Preciate it."

Working slowly, Stine poured the coffee. As he turned and handed it to Dan Colt, he said, "Have you traveled far, Mr. Sundeen?"

The young deputy was obviously stalling for time. It was all right with Dan. He would rather talk to the sheriff.

"Quite a stretch," Dan said idly. He would purposely keep the conversation low-key until the sheriff's arrival.

"From what direction?"

"Northeast."

"You been lookin' for your brother?"

"Yep," said Dan, sipping politely at the bitter black liquid.

"Long time?"

"Quite awhile."

Young Stine was searching for another question when the hollow sound of boots on the boardwalk met his ears.

Dan set the cup on the desk and stood up as John Springer entered, Pardee at his heels.

"Mr. Sundeen," said Stine quickly, "this is Sheriff John Springer."

The sheriff did not hear what Stine said. His eyes widened as he focused on Dan's face. "How—"

"This is Dave's twin brother, Sheriff," said Stine.

"Twin brother!" ejaculated Slim Pardee, slapping a palm to his face.

Dan extended his hand and briefly clasped Springer's.

"S–sit down, Mr. Sundeen," stammered the sheriff.

Dan returned to his chair, noticing that people were gathering in the street, trying to see in.

"Close the door, Slim," commanded Springer, lowering his muscular frame into the desk chair.

Pardee closed the door and walked to the rear of John Springer, joining Stine. All three lawmen studied Dan's face.

"Unbelievable," breathed Springer. "Unbelievable."

"I didn't tell him anything, Mr. Springer," said Ralph Stine.

A glum look spread over Springer's face. Looking Colt in the eye, he said, "I have bad news for you, Mr. Sundeen. Your brother is dead."

Dan's face stiffened. His heart skipped a beat. A cold wave of horror washed over him.

"Bushwacker shot him in the back. We buried him two days ago."

Dan's mind was whirling, seething, struggling to grasp the meaning of the words he was hearing. Without Dave he would never convince Logan Tanner or any other representative of the law that he was innocent. His face was pinched and gray.

"I'm sorry," said Springer. "I'm sure you and Dave were close. It's a loss for me too. He saved my life a couple weeks ago. Stepped in to help me against four gunmen. They shot me, here in the shoulder. He killed all four of them."

Dan was shocked but pleased to know that Dave would side with a lawman.

"I'm glad to know that," said Dan softly. Standing up, he said, "I assume he's at Boot Hill."

"Yessir," replied Springer. "I can ride out with you—"

"No, thanks," Dan said, managing a smile. "I'd rather go alone."

Reaching the door, the tall man turned. "Any personal effects?"

"Nossir," said Springer. "He's buried in a pine coffin. We just left his clothes and guns on him. Even left his hat with him."

"Horse? Saddle?"

"Hostler sold them this morning," answered the sheriff. "Said a drifter came through needing a horse. Said Dave owed him. Price he got was just enough to square the bill."

John Springer followed Dan outside. As the blond man swung into the saddle, the lawman said, "You going to be around long?"

"No need to hang around," replied Colt. "Probably pull out in the morning."

"If there's anything I can do, Mr. Sundeen, you just name it," said Springer tenderly. "Anything."

"Thanks, Sheriff," said Dan. "I'll let you know."

The crowd had scattered when Dan emerged through the door. Pallid, frightened faces watched from the sidewalks in utter silence as the black gelding trotted out of town.

The rim of the sun was barely visible on the western horizon as Dan Colt slipped his left foot from the stirrup and walked toward the fresh mound. A heavy hopelessness hung over him like a lurid pall as he read the inscription on the gravemarker.

Fate's foul hand had dealt him a final, wicked blow. Dan Colt must live as a haunted fugitive for the rest of his earthly life. There was no way to prove— His thoughts jammed. Wait a minute! Even his brother's corpse would prove to Tanner and the judge who sent him to Yuma that there was a twin! That was it! He would ask Springer for permission to exhume the body.

It was dark when Dan alighted from the black gelding and crossed the boardwalk. Tombstone's sheriff was bent over his desk, reading the latest issue of the Tombstone *Epitaph*.

BOOT HILL BROTHER   205

Springer looked up as the tall man entered. The lantern on the desk flickered as a momentary breeze stirred the stagnant air in the office.

"Hello, Sundeen," Springer said, smiling. "I was just reading about the big robbery. Couple days ago a gang of outlaws posing as a cavalry escort robbed Wells Fargo of half a million dollars. Railroad payroll." Shaking his head, he ejected a low whistle. "Things'll be hot over in Tucson for a while."

"You said if I need any favors . . ." Dan said softly.

"You bet, Sundeen. Name it. Your brother saved my life. Anything you—"

"I want permission to dig up Dave's body."

Springer's face tightened. "I'm sorry, Sundeen, but I can't allow that."

"Why not?" asked Dan indignantly. "He was my brother."

John Springer repeated his refusal, explaining that Boot Hill burials were different from those in the regular cemetery. Once interred, the body became the property of the county. The situation was now irreversible.

As the sheriff went through his wordy explanation, Dan's thoughts rambled. At first he thought he should tell the whole story to the lawman. Certainly Springer would understand his predicament. Exhuming Dave's body would clear him with the law. Yuma Prison would no longer be a threat. He could roam the country a free man. *But why should I have to tell the story?* he thought. *Certainly a man has a right to claim his own brother's body and give it a proper burial in a respectable cemetery.*

Dan argued his case on the proper-burial basis but to no avail. Springer was sorry, but it was a closed matter. Dan left the office, anger welling up inside him. His freedom was pitted against a bureaucratic rule.

Mounting the black gelding, the angry Colt rode up Allen to Fourth Street and turned right. At Fourth and Fremont an elderly man stood beside an old, dilapidated wagon. By the light of two lanterns he had placed on the ground, he was trying to slip a rear wheel onto the axle. The wiry little man was filling the cool night air with cuss words.

Reining in next to the crippled vehicle, the tall man said, "Need some help, old-timer?"

The old codger tossed Dan a quick glance. "Sure could use a little, sonny," he answered with a crackly voice. "Stupid blacksmith took all afternoon to fix the rim on this wheel, then closed up and left me to put it back on by myself."

Only then did Dan notice the sign on the blacksmith shop.

The bony nag harnessed to the wagon swished her tail and nickered at the black gelding.

Dismounting, Dan observed that the bed of the wagon was littered with tools, along with a few sacks of flour and other articles. The suspended corner of the wagon was supported by several blocks of wood, which had settled somewhat in the soft earth during the repair of the iron rim on the wheel. The wagon would have to be hoisted about two inches.

Stepping to the center of the wagon at the tailgate, Dan curled his fingers under the edge and braced his feet. "Okay, pop," he said, "when I lift, you shove it on."

The wagon rose freely and the old man slipped the wheel on the axle. The lock nut was soon tightened in place. Wiping axle grease from his hands with an old rag, the wiry little man said, "I'm beholdin' to you, sonny."

"Glad to oblige," said Dan.

"Name's Clete Devlin," said the old man, extending a bony hand.

"Dan Colt," replied the tall man.

Cocking his head and squinting at Dan's face, he said, "You ain't an angel are yuh?"

Dan chuckled. "Why would you ask that?"

" 'Cuz I heered angels have golden hair like your'n."

"Well, if I was, pop, you'd be in trouble," Dan said with a wry grin.

"How's that?" Devlin's voice crackled.

"The way you were cussin', if I was an angel, I'da kicked those blocks of wood out from under that wagon."

Devlin's face flushed. The light from the lanterns twinkled in his eyes. "I only cuss when I'm mad," he said curtly.

"You just passing through?" Dan asked, showing interest.

"Yep. Been prospectin' out Californy way. Luck ain't been so hot. Me and Zeldie Mae—that's my horse—air headin' for the Rockies. Hear there's gold up by Leadville."

"You going right now or in the morning?"

"Plan to pull over behind the livery. Sleep in the wagon. Move on about sunup."

"You wouldn't rent a fella a shovel, some rope, and a lantern for a couple hours, would you?"

"Wouldn't rent 'em. But shore would loan 'em."

"Thanks, pop. I'll have them back in a little while," said Dan, lifting a sturdy shovel from the wagon bed. Picking up a length of rope and a lantern, he doused the light, mounted, and faded into the night.

CHAPTER NINETEEN

Ric Baron awoke with a start. The room was dark. Music from one of the saloons was filtering through the open window. A light breeze rustled the curtains.

His stomach reminded him that the last meal had been too long ago. Pulling on his boots in the dark, he stood up, lifted the guns from the bedpost, and buckled the belt. He tied the thongs adeptly, donned his hat, and left the room.

The clock on the lobby wall advised Baron that it would be ten o'clock in six minutes. The Great Western dining room had been closed since eight o'clock, but Baron's persistence garnered him a meal of cold leftovers.

During the meal the slender gunslinger reminded himself that he had one more trip to Boot Hill. One more mockery of Dave Sundeen's grave would fulfill his promise to his dead brother. The thought of Boot Hill this late at night was repelling to his sensitive nature, but to wait till morning would not effectuate his promise to the letter. He must go the grave before midnight. The insane, wild look came again to his eyes.

An old man was tinkering in the bed of a dilapidated wagon by lanternlight as Ric Baron reined his horse into the alley behind the livery stable.

* * *

Dan Colt placed his hat over the pommel and ground-reined the black gelding on the blind side of the Boot Hill cemetery. It was after ten o'clock. He doubted that anyone would be on the road this late, but if the gelding smelled another horse, it would nicker. With him behind the hill, this would not be a problem.

Dan had hoped he could dig without using the light, but clouds had covered the moon soon after its rising. He would need the aid of the lantern. Shielding the match flame from the wind, Dan touched it to the wick.

The lantern made an eerie glow in the cemetery. Light gusts of wind teased the flame, causing long shadows to dance over the graves.

Dan rocked the gravemarker back and forth until it slipped free from the sod. The soft earth offered no resistance to the shovel. In a short time he was standing chest-deep in the hole. The dirt was piled on the low side of the grave, opposite the road.

The noise of the shovel scraping on the top of the coffin prevented Dan from hearing the approach of Ric Baron's horse. Baron dismounted at the entrance, leaving the horse standing in the dark.

As the slender gunman wove his way carefully in the near pitch-blackness, Dan discarded the shovel and squatted in the grave, brushing dirt from the top of the coffin. The lantern stood on the same side of the yawning hole that Ric was approaching.

The flickering flame caught Baron's gaze at about twenty yards. He blinked and rubbed his eyes. Edging closer, he swallowed hard. He wanted to turn and run, but something within drove him forward.

At ten yards Ric could see that the grave was open. His heart pounded savagely. He could feel the pulse throbbing in his temples. *Turn and run!* he told himself. The nameless force within him was unyielding.

Baron wanted to wipe the cold sweat from his face, but his hands refused to move. Only his legs seemed functional.

As he stepped within ten feet of the grave, Dan slowly stood up. The light of the lantern fully exposed his face. The wind tousled his blond locks.

To Ric Baron, Dan appeared to be floating out of the grave.

Startled, Dan fixed his ice-blue stare on the slender youth, instantly recognizing him in the pale light. "Looking for *me*, Ric?"

Baron's face froze. His eyes widened, struck with fear. His mouth went dry. A sharp pain ripped through his chest, followed by an inky-black numbness. He collapsed in a rumpled heap.

Quickly Dan Colt climbed from the grave. Placing the lantern beside the still form of the young gunman, he straightened the shoulders and lifted his head. *Ric Baron was dead.*

Instantly Dan comprehended. It was Ric who had shot Dave in the back, thinking he was Dan. For some unknown reason the kid had come to visit the grave. Not knowing there was a twin, he thought the dead man was coming for him from the grave. The dreadful shock was too much for his heart.

The dead youth's eyes were open, bulging. Dan tried to close them. They seemed frozen, too large for their sockets.

Leaving the corpse to the darkness, Dan returned to his brother's grave. Having made room for the rope around the coffin, he looped it over the end where he assumed the head would be. Once again on solid ground he exerted the strength in his muscular legs, back, and arms.

Dan was breathing heavily when the heavy box teetered on the edge of the hole, then leveled on the ground with a soft thud. Jamming the sharp point of

Clete Devlin's shovel under the edge of the lid, he pried it upward. The nails resisted with a grating sound and then gave way. The lid swung loose and clattered to the sod. Dan could not see into the coffin without the light.

As he leaned over to grasp the lantern, his heart was in his throat. He had only a hazy, vague recollection of ever seeing his twin. It had been over thirty years. Seeing him now . . . this way . . . would only result in bitter frustration. There was no choice. It had to be done.

Taking a deep breath of the cool night air, Dan lifted the lantern over the coffin. His mouth fell open. *Four saddle bags lay in disorderly fashion on a heap of fist-size stones!*

A wave of relief rushed over Dan Colt's body. Maybe Dave was not dead! Even his corpse would have cleared Dan of all charges, but somehow that didn't matter. Dave was his brother—more: his *twin*. No matter what he had done or what he was, Dan loved him. He would have to capture Dave one day. Turn him in to the law. Clear his own name. But for the moment the tall man felt nothing but relief. There was a chance. Dave might still be alive!

Fumbling with the straps on the saddle bags, the blond man found numerous packages of brand-new neatly packed bills. There was also an envelope containing a breakdown of the various denominations, which totaled $505,450.00, plus a copy of a receipt for that amount made out to the First National Bank of Tucson and signed by a Harry Forbes.

Suddenly the night wind carried the sound of boots scraping on loose dirt. Dan's head snapped upward. His eyes settled on three indistinct forms standing on the outer edge of the circle of light provided by the lantern.

Dan straightened, letting the saddle bag slip from his fingers and fall into the coffin. Two of the forms moved into the light, halting some twelve or fourteen feet from where the tall man stood. One was Mack Evans, whose massive frame appeared especially huge against the black background. The other was Otis Becker, a big man, but small when he stood next to Evans. Dan Colt had never seen either one before. Both were pointing revolvers at him.

Evans's ponderous voice filled the night. "Looks like Dave's brother has a big nose, boss," he said, turning his head slightly. He was addressing the third man, who remained in the background.

"Looks like he's got his grave all dug," said Becker huskily. "All we gotta do is kill 'im and plant 'im in it."

The third man stepped between Becker and Evans. The badge on his vest glittered briefly when it caught the light.

John Springer spoke solemnly. "I told you to leave the grave alone. Now it will be yours." The sheriff's right hand also held a gun.

Cold rage pulsated through Dan Colt. "Where's my brother?" he said through his teeth.

Ignoring the question, Springer said evenly, "You were just about to mess up a good thing."

"The only thing I hate more than a hypocrite preacher is a crooked lawman," hissed Dan. "I take it you're the mastermind behind this Fargo caper."

"I don't mind telling a dead man," said Springer haughtily. "I have a connection in the Fargo organization. With his help—for a cut of the take, of course—we're doing pretty good." Looking toward the coffin, he continued. "This was the big one. Your brother helped us pull it off."

"While you hid behind a badge and pulled the strings," Dan said, lips drawn tight.

"Can you think of a safer place?" Springer asked, chuckling. "After all, if you can't trust your sheriff . . . who can you trust?"

Stepping back two spaces, Springer said coldly, *"Kill 'im."*

Dan knew there was only one way out.

It would take a full second for them to squeeze triggers. The swiftness of the tall, blond gunslinger cut the time in half. Both Colts roared before either bulky man could fire. Dan flung a third shot into the darkness between them.

Otis Becker's heart exploded with the bullet's impact. He was dead before he hit the ground. Evans's big body flinched and reeled heavily, the unfired gun sliding from his fingers.

As a precautionary measure Dan slammed two more bullets in the direction of the invisible sheriff.

Mack Evans hit the earth with a thud and rolled over. Dan thought he was dead when the wounded monster reached out, clawing at the ground for his gun. Finding it, he swung it toward Colt.

"Don't do it!" Dan shouted. He was keeping to the outside rim of the circle of light until he was sure Springer was out of commission.

Evans thumbed back the hammer. Dan's left-hand gun belched orange flame. Evans let out a grunt, dropping the gun, as his big head thumped the ground. Dan stepped forward and kicked the gun from the huge man's reach.

Quickly he moved toward the spot where he had last seen Springer. Tombstone's crooked sheriff would mastermind no more crimes. The first shot had gotten him—right in the mouth. Apparently he had gone into a crouch. Dan had aimed for his chest.

Mack Evans moaned. Moving to him, Colt knelt down. In the yellow light the death mask on the giant's face was evident.

"Mister, you're dying. Do a decent thing, will you?" Dan pleaded.

Evans rolled his tongue around his thick lips. He looked at Dan with glassy eyes.

"Where's my brother?" Dan asked frantically.

Evans rolled his tongue again. His breathing was unsteady. Two crimson spots were spreading on his chest. "He's . . ." The dying man swallowed painfully. "He's . . . in . . . Mexico. Nogales. Wounded bad. Black man . . ." Evans coughed. "Black man took him . . . in wagon. Town thinks . . . thinks he died. Boss let him go. Grave . . . was perfect . . . perfect place . . . to . . . hide money."

"What's the black man's name?"

"James. . ." Evans coughed again, drew a breath, and let it out. It was his last.

Dan Colt prepared to ride out of Tombstone after telling the story to Stine and Pardee over breakfast. He would personally deliver the half-million dollars to the bank in Tucson for safekeeping until Wells Fargo could make arrangements to transport it to Phoenix.

At first the deputies objected to his carrying it alone until Dan convinced them that a lone rider would be less conspicuous.

Clete Devlin was still asleep behind the livery stable. Dan quietly deposited the borrowed articles in the rear of the wagon and spurred the big black gelding toward Tucson. He would get this task over with, then head for Nogales. If Dave's wound were as serious as it sounded, he would be there for quite a while.

Pressing the gelding hard, the tall man rode into Tucson at one thirty. With a pair of stuffed saddle bags on each shoulder, he strode into the First National Bank. Two tellers were on duty behind the brass bars. One had a customer. Dan spoke to the other. "Got a few dollars here to deposit. Belongs to Wells Fargo."

The middle-aged man cast a casual glance at the saddle bags. Suddenly he recognized them. His eyes widened. Fixing them on Don's face, he said, "Mr. Sparkman is out of the bank at the moment, sir."

"Sparkman?"

"He's the president, sir. He'll be the one to talk to."

"When will he be back?"

"Well, I—"

"He's over at the sheriff's office right now," interrupted the other teller, whose customer had left. "Wells Fargo executives are over there with him. They just arrived from Denver."

"Is *all* the money there?" asked the first teller.

"As far as I know," said Dan flatly.

The second teller spoke again. "They should know right now."

"If you gentlemen will lock this money in the safe, I'll go tell them," said Colt quietly.

"Yessir, yessir!" said the first teller, grasping the saddle bags as Dan hoisted them over the bars.

"Sheriff's office is—"

"I know where it is," said Dan, heading for the door.

Moments later the big black gelding felt Dan Colt's two-hundred-and-ten-pound frame ease off its back in front of the sheriff's office.

The door was open. Heavy conversation was in progress. Dan's muscular form filled the doorway, demanding the immediate attention of the occupants. The conversation halted abruptly.

A tall, narrow-shouldered man of sixty, wearing a star, stood up. "Help you, mister?" he said in a friendly tone.

"I understand there's a Mr. Sparkman here," said Dan.

"I'm Leonard Sparkman," said a well-dressed, distinguished-looking man, rising to his feet.

"I just delivered four saddle bags containing a half-million dollars to your bank," the blond man said calmly.

The two remaining men leaped to their feet. One of them asked excitedly, "Are you talking about the money from the robbery?"

"The same."

Pandemonium broke loose. Everyone was firing questions at once. The sheriff was able to calm them and restore order after several moments. Sitting down with Dan Colt in a central position, they listened intently as he told the story. Dan was just finishing when one of the bank tellers entered.

"Mr. Sparkman," he said excitedly, eyes dancing, "I thought you would want to know that all the money that was stolen is there. We counted all the packets. Unless someone slipped bills out of the packets, we haven't lost a dollar. It will take us awhile to give a definite word on that."

"Thank you, Higgins," said Sparkman. "I'll be back to the bank shortly."

Higgins disappeared.

The Wells Fargo executives introduced themselves to Dan as William Brown and David Hanna.

The slender sheriff extended his hand. "I'm Owen Darby, sir. You haven't told us *your* name."

Squeezing the lawman's raw-boned hand, Dan said, "Colt. Dan Colt."

The sheriff's mouth came open. He eyed the low-slung .45's. "The gunslinger?"

"Yep."

"I thought—"

"So did a lot of people," Dan interjected. "You can see it isn't so."

Darby squinted. "You look familiar. Have we met before?"

"It's possible," said Dan. He thought of Dave's face on the well-circulated posters. "Ever been in Denver?"

"Several times."

"Probably there," Dan said, avoiding direct eye contact.

"Maybe so."

Dan hoped the diversion would hold long enough for him to put some desert between himself and Tucson.

"Well, gentlemen, I've gotta ride," advised Dan.

"Hold it, Colt," said William Brown.

Dan flashed him a wary glance.

"You can't just ride away," Brown said, his face expressionless.

"Oh?" The tall man's heart beat hard.

"Wells Fargo just posted a reward for information leading to the arrest of the robbers. You've done us one better." Brown's face broke into a radiant smile. "You brought us the money."

Colt's nerves relaxed. "Just doing my duty as a citizen," he said quietly.

"The reward is ten thousand dollars, Mr. Colt," said Brown.

Dan's blue eyes seemed to come alive. His brain was spinning.

"However," continued the Fargo executive, "since we apparently have recovered the full amount, I have the authority to show Wells Fargo's appreciation by raising the reward. I'm doubling it. Twenty thousand."

A broad grin spread over Dan Colt's handsome suntanned face. "That's mighty generous of you, Mr. Brown."

"Not really, when you think about it," mused

Brown, raising his eyebrows. "You *could* have had half a million!"

Laughter erupted among the happy men.

"I can draw a draft on our account at Mr. Sparkman's bank, or you can have cash," Brown said warmly.

Dan Colt's mind had already begun doing some calculating.

"Would you mind, sir," said Dan, "if we made a draft in someone else's name for fifteen thousand? I'll take the rest in cash."

"Fine," said Brown, fishing in his coat for something to write on.

The raw-boned sheriff went to his desk and quickly returned with pencil and paper.

"Mr. Sparkman needs to get back to the bank," said Brown, his pencil poised over the paper. "We'll have him prepare the draft while Hanna and I take you over to the hotel for a meal. You look hungry."

Dan smiled. "Come to think of it, I am," he said.

"To whom do we make the draft? *Mrs.* Colt, perhaps?"

"No, sir," said Dan calmly. "She's dead, sir."

"Oh, forgive me, I—"

"It's all right, sir, how would you know?"

Brown's face flushed. "To whom do we make it?" he asked, pencil ready.

"Clara Wyler," Dan answered, feeling warm all over. "W-y-l-e-r."

After Sparkman had left, the Fargo men talked briefly with the sheriff. Dan slipped through the door and waited on the boardwalk. He heard Owen Darby laugh as he followed the two executives through the door. "Tanner is gonna be madder'n a wet hen when word gets to him!"

Echoing the sheriff's laughter, David Hanna agreed, "You can bet on that!"

The name *Tanner* stuck in Dan's mind. Casually he eyed Darby and said, "What's the joke?"

"United States Marshal," said Darby, "Logan Tanner. He was passing through here heading to Tombstone when the big robbery took place. Chasing some convict who escaped Yuma."

"Oh?" Dan's insides were churning.

"Tanner's superiors told him to follow up on the robbery. Cavalry officer who was leading the escort told Tanner the gang headed north."

David Hanna laughed again. "Hot-headed dude's probably in Idaho by now!"

CHAPTER TWENTY

The sun was dropping low in the western sky when Dan Colt momentarily halted the black horse at the gate of the Wyler ranch. A white sign with perfect black letters was fastened to the gate post:

> RANCH FOR SALE
> *Inquire Within*

Clucking to the gelding, Dan guided him through the gate and down the grassy slope. The leaves in the cottonwood trees flickered little glints of sunlight as the afternoon breeze frolicked across the valley.

Randy Wyler was the first to spot the approaching rider. He was listlessly beating a rug that hung on the clothesline beside the house.

The boy focused on the tall, erect form in the saddle, then briefly eyed the horse. Dropping the rug-beater, he raced toward the house. "Mama! Mama!" he shouted at the top of his lungs, "It's Dan! It's Dan Colt!"

As horse and rider sauntered into the yard, Clara bounded through the door, drying her hands on an apron.

"Dan! You came back!" she cried. "Did you find your brother?"

Descending stiffly from the saddle, the tall man held the small woman briefly in his arms, then with one hand he tousled Randy's hair. "No, ma'am," Dan answered. "I didn't find him. I know where he is though. He's recuperating from a gunshot wound in Nogales."

"Weren't you in Tombstone?" Clara asked, brushing a lock of hair from her eyes.

"Yes."

"That's so close to Nogales. Why—?"

"I had to come back. I see you haven't sold the place."

As Clara shook her head in acknowledgment, Dan's eye caught sight of Dolly slipping through the door and limping toward him. It was evident that the delay of her appearance was for a few moments of facial preparation.

"Hello, Dan!" she cried warmly, gliding into his arms.

"How's my gal?" he asked, squeezing till she grunted.

"Just fine."

Dan looked at Clara. "Pop? Molly Jo?"

"Molly Jo is staying with a woman who was recently widowed. She has no family, so Molly Jo is going to live with her for a month or so. Place is north about forty miles. Pop just took her. He'll be back tomorrow." Clara cocked her head sideways. "You said you had to come back."

"Yes'm." Dan was still holding the crippled girl.

"Well, come on in the house and tell us about it," the small woman said, tugging at his arm.

"I really can't, Clara," the tall man said apologetically. "I have got to turn right around and head for Nogales. Every minute counts."

Clara Wyler's face twisted slightly. "But what—?"

Dan released Dolly and walked to the big horse. From the saddle bag he produced a white envelope.

Returning to face the mother, he pulled the girl to his side with one arm. "That doctor still in Denver?"

"Why, yes," Clara said, her eyes quizzical.

"I did a little favor for the Wells Fargo people down in Tucson. There was a reward attached to it. Drifter like me doesn't need much money."

Extending the envelope to Clara, Dan said, "This will fix it so you can burn that sign on the gate and take my gal, here, to Denver."

As Clara's trembling fingers opened the envelope, Dan said, "Oughtta be enough to keep you in style in Denver until Dolly's healed and ready to come home."

The petite lady's eyes filled with tears as she beheld the draft. Her lower lip quivered. She reversed the draft so that Dolly could see it. The girl burst into tears, wrapping both arms around Dan Colt's slender waist.

When the two females had gained control of themselves, Dan embraced them one more time, shook hands with Randy, and swung into the saddle.

"You come back, Dan Colt, you hear me?" said Clara.

"Someday, ma'am."

"*Please*," sobbed Dolly.

"When I do, you're gonna walk to me, just like all the other girls walk," said Dan.

The hot lump in Dolly's throat choked off her words.

Dan touched the brim of his Stetson. "Bye."

The three Wylers followed him to the edge of the yard, halting where the double-rutted wagon trail bit into the grass. Each, through their own wall of tears, watched quietly until Dan Colt crested the hill at the gate.

He paused at the gate, leaned from the saddle, and removed the sign from the post. Dropping it earthward, he guided the horse onto the road. For a brief moment the broad-shouldered man was silhouetted against the bloodred sky.

Then he was gone.

Dell Bestsellers

- [ ] **RANDOM WINDS** by Belva Plain ....$3.50 **(17158-X)**
- [ ] **MEN IN LOVE** by Nancy Friday ....$3.50 **(15404-9)**
- [ ] **JAILBIRD** by Kurt Vonnegut ....$3.25 **(15447-2)**
- [ ] **LOVE: Poems** by Danielle Steel ....$2.50 **(15377-8)**
- [ ] **SHOGUN** by James Clavell ....$3.50 **(17800-2)**
- [ ] **WILL** by G. Gordon Liddy ....$3.50 **(09666-9)**
- [ ] **THE ESTABLISHMENT** by Howard Fast........$3.25 **(12296-1)**
- [ ] **LIGHT OF LOVE** by Barbara Cartland ....$2.50 **(15402-2)**
- [ ] **SERPENTINE** by Thomas Thompson ....$3.50 **(17611-5)**
- [ ] **MY MOTHER/MY SELF** by Nancy Friday ....$3.25 **(15663-7)**
- [ ] **EVERGREEN** by Belva Plain ....$3.50 **(13278-9)**
- [ ] **THE WINDSOR STORY**
  by J. Bryan III & Charles J.V. Murphy ....$3.75 **(19346-X)**
- [ ] **THE PROUD HUNTER** by Marianne Harvey ..$3.25 **(17098-2)**
- [ ] **HIT ME WITH A RAINBOW**
  by James Kirkwood ....$3.25 **(13622-9)**
- [ ] **MIDNIGHT MOVIES** by David Kaufelt ....$2.75 **(15728-5)**
- [ ] **THE DEBRIEFING** by Robert Litell ....$2.75 **(01873-5)**
- [ ] **SHAMAN'S DAUGHTER** by Nan Salerno
  & Rosamond Vanderburgh ....$3.25 **(17863-0)**
- [ ] **WOMAN OF TEXAS** by R.T. Stevens ....$2.95 **(19555-1)**
- [ ] **DEVIL'S LOVE** by Lane Harris ....$2.95 **(11915-4)**

At your local bookstore or use this handy coupon for ordering:

Dell | **DELL BOOKS
P.O. BOX 1000, PINEBROOK, N.J. 07058**

Please send me the books I have checked above. I am enclosing $ _____
(please add 75¢ per copy to cover postage and handling). Send check or money order—no cash or C.O.D.'s. Please allow up to 8 weeks for shipment.

Mr/Mrs/Miss _____

Address _____

City _____ State/Zip _____